"You tempt me, Daniel Pendleton," Sara said, seeing sensual recognition in his gaze.

She paused, then went on. "You make me think about what I'm missing, about what it's like to hold and be held. To spend a night so lost in pleasure that night turns to day and day turns to night." She bit her lip, appalled at all she'd revealed, horrified at what she'd admitted. "But you're a good man, Daniel. And I'm not going to ruin any more good men. I'm not going to ruin you."

Daniel felt even more determined to have her. That she wanted to protect him was precious, but that she thought he was an angel was a problem. "What if I'm not all that good?"

She smiled. "If being responsible were a crime, you'd get life in prison."

"Don't rub it in. Because I had to raise my brothers and sister, I never got to do what I wanted. Never got to sow my oats, or go parking on a Saturday night." A dangerous light came into his eyes. "Every man needs to have one fling with a wild woman."

He took her hand and kissed her palm, the warmth of his lips kindling her nerve endings. As his tongue darted out to taste the tender skin of her wrist, Sara felt her breath squeezed from her lungs.

"I can handle the risk, honey," he said in a low, husky voice. "Ruin me. . . ."

WHAT ARE *LOVESWEPT* ROMANCES?

They are stories of true romance and touching emotion. We believe those two very important ingredients are constants in our highly sensual and very believable stories in the LOVESWEPT line. Our goal is to give you, the reader, stories of consistently high quality that may sometimes make you laugh, sometimes make you cry, but are always fresh and creative and contain many delightful surprises within their pages.

Most romance fans read an enormous number of books. Those they truly love, they keep. Others may be traded with friends and soon forgotten. We hope that each LOVESWEPT romance will be a treasure—a "keeper." We will always try to publish

LOVE STORIES YOU'LL NEVER FORGET
BY AUTHORS YOU'LL ALWAYS REMEMBER

The Editors

Loveswept ®673

MORE THAN A MISTRESS

LEANNE BANKS

BANTAM BOOKS

NEW YORK · TORONTO · LONDON · SYDNEY · AUCKLAND

MORE THAN A MISTRESS
A Bantam Book / March 1994

If you would be interested in receiving protective vinyl covers for your
Loveswept books, please write to this address for information:

Loveswept
Bantam Books
P.O. Box 985
Hicksville, NY 11802

ISBN 0-553-44383-6

Published simultaneously in the United States and Canada

This book is dedicated to
everyone who ever wondered if they
were good enough . . . for love.

PROLOGUE

She wore a red silk slip.

The military would have called that slip a smart weapon because the vibrant undergarment didn't miss a single one of her lethal feminine curves, from high-thrusting breasts to a slim waist down to inviting hips.

Daniel's hands itched to trace those curves, to slide his hands into her long, tousled brown hair and bring her closer so that he could taste her mouth.

Her hazel eyes glinted gold in the wavering candlelight, and he could read the message in Sara Kingston's gaze. She wanted him. At last.

His heart raced as he reached for her. She was soft and warm, everything he'd ever wanted. He pushed the red slip down her shoulders and pulled her closer, catching his breath at the sensation of her breasts nestling against his chest.

He kissed her, stealing her little gasp. Daniel wasn't sure who was leading whom in this voyage of pleasure, but at the moment he felt too good to care.

He lifted one of her hands to his lips and noticed how small it seemed within his larger one.

"Fragile."

Sara's lips tilted in sultry, mesmerizing invitation. She moved back slightly and slid her fingers down his chest to his abdomen. "Capable."

Daniel's gut tightened. He knew what was coming.

Sara, with the sweet, sexy smile, wrapped her fragile, yet capable hand around him and stroked.

He groaned, feeling the breath back up in his chest. He swelled within her hand, the familiar punch of arousal flooding his blood. She brought him so much pleasure, but he felt the slightest edge of panic. She'd touched him before, brought him to the edge time and time again, only to leave him wanting.

He sensed her resistance to him was something she couldn't help. It was there shadowing her eyes, the sadness and the wanting. She wanted more, but something stopped her.

He reached for her shoulders when she began to fade away. "Stop! Don't go. For God's sake, don't leave me this time."

Her gaze grew tormented. "I don't know. I'm just not sure."

Daniel kissed her. "Be sure. I want you so much."

He saw the dreaded word forming on her mouth and kissed her again.

"Don't say no this time." He'd heard her say it so many times. It was like the lash of a whip across his soul. He needed her. He didn't understand why, he just knew he did. "Say yes. I'll take care of you."

Flashes of uncertainty came and went in her eyes. "Are you sure?" Her voice was small, almost childlike.

His heart turned over, and he dragged her closer, his hands caressing her thighs and seeking the treasure of her arousal. "Yes, but I need to hear you say the word. Just one little word, Sara."

Tentatively she moved over him, her hair swinging in a soft, fragrant curtain to his shoulders. She licked her lips, seeming to take courage.

"So close, Sara," he coaxed, swallowing past the dryness in his throat. "Just say the word."

"I want you."

"Say it," he muttered in a rough voice.

She hovered for a moment, then her eyes lit up. "Yes," she whispered and eased onto him. "Yesss."

Something tight and achy burst free in his

chest. His excitement went beyond the physical. Her affirmative answer meant she accepted and trusted him. It meant that her feelings for him were stronger than what lurked in the shadows. They stared at each other, and he laughed at how utterly invincible he felt. He'd never been this excited in his life.

Daniel didn't know which sent him running, tumbling over the edge: the way she clasped him inside her or that she'd finally said yes to him. Finally.

He raced down a track of sensation, a freight train roaring in his head, as he struggled to hold on to Sara. But her image bled away. His heart pounded furiously and his lungs screamed for oxygen. His release was powerful, shattering, propelled by too many nights of wanting and not having.

Shudders racked his body, his hands clasping and unclasping. But it wasn't sweet Sara's skin he touched. It was the cotton sheet on his bed.

Daniel's eyes flew open.

He was so disoriented, it took several deep breaths before he recognized his room. His familiar furniture seemed oddly out of place. Where were the candles? Where was Sara?

The night air cooled him quickly.

"Damn," he muttered, pushing aside the sheet and sitting on the side of the bed. Resting his elbows on his knees, he slid his hands through his hair in complete bewilderment. Another dream, Lord help him.

He let out a long, heavy sigh and shook his head. Oh, sure, this one had been different. This time she'd said yes, and she'd given him a measure of physical release.

His body was somewhat appeased, but his spirit wasn't.

Wearily he rose from the bed and followed his usual routine. He trudged to the connecting bathroom, stepped into the shower, and jerked the cold-water faucet on full force. His body quivered, rebelling in shock. Something had to be done. He couldn't continue this way.

At thirty-five, Daniel Pendleton knew himself well. He knew what other people saw when they looked at him—a hardworking, upstanding, responsible citizen. The eldest of seven brothers and one sister, he'd managed the family farm since his father had died years ago. His father's death had taken away his opportunity to go to college, which still brought a sting of disappointment and regret. Daniel, however, wasn't the type to wallow in misery. He set his mind on something and got the job done.

He'd been involved with a few women, but he'd always made it clear that he wasn't interested in forever. His family obligations had stripped him clean of any desire for more permanent connections.

Daniel turned the faucet off and reached for a towel, thinking that he'd been reasonably pleased with his life until lately. Until Sara Kingston had taken up residence in his dreams. He scowled, scrubbing his chilled body with the towel.

He wasn't happy with his present state. Discontent had been rumbling in his gut, making him irritable, which wasn't the norm for him. His family would say Daniel wasn't difficult to please. His sister would claim he was her most easygoing brother. His friends would say he was the kind of man you could depend on.

There were things his family didn't know about him, though. Things nobody knew about him. When something got in his way, Daniel could be ruthless. Nobody knew it, because nobody had been stupid enough to get in his way.

Now there was Sara. She taunted and teased him night after night. She'd gotten into his blood like a fever no antibiotic could treat. *He wanted her.*

Daniel balled up the towel and crammed it into the clothes hamper. He'd given himself time to get over this foolishness, but time hadn't done the trick.

Glancing at the luminescent numbers on his

alarm clock, he felt resolution harden within him like steel. It was time, once and for all, to get Sara Kingston out of his system.

There was only one way to do it. He would have to take her to bed.

ONE

"No," Sara said, softening the rejection with her most polite smile. "It's nice of you to ask, but I really need to check on the appetizers." She backed away, hoping she hadn't offended the client, but something about the way the man looked at her made her uneasy. She shouldn't have worn that red slip tonight.

Sara rolled her eyes. Paranoid! The man wasn't Superman. It wasn't as if he could see what kind of underwear she was wearing.

She checked the well-stocked linen-covered tables. Her boss, Carly Bradford, had pulled out all the stops and thrown a huge Christmas party aboard *Matilda's Dream*, the riverboat Carly owned and hired out for parties. Travel agents, local business representatives, and Carly's seven brothers danced, dined, laughed, and flirted on the three decorated decks. Not being one for social affairs, Sara had tried to beg off, but Carly was more than a boss. She was a friend, and she seemed determined to include Sara in every family event.

"You make a career of checking on the appetizers," a deep male voice said from behind her.

Sara stiffened. Daniel Pendleton. Ever since she'd accidentally spilled soup in his lap six months ago, he'd made her feel about as desirable as coffee dregs. Daniel had burned his hands in a barn fire, and Carly had asked Sara to help take care of him. Daniel hadn't been the least bit grateful. Their relationship was at best civil.

Sara took a calming breath and inhaled the faint scent of sandalwood and soap. She turned to face Daniel. "Carly's busy keeping everyone entertained. I'm just trying to be useful."

"Thought Carly said she wanted the staff to take the night off and act like guests." He gestured toward a waiter outfitted in black. "She even got a temp agency to provide waitstaff." His mouth tilted into a grin. "You're supposed to be having fun."

The white slash of his teeth disconcerted her. "I—"

"Wanna dance?"

Surprised at the invitation, Sara blinked, then automatically shook her head. "No," she managed. "I—"

"Why?"

She stared into his trademark Pendleton violet eyes and drew a complete blank.

If a name had to be put after the word *masculine* in the dictionary, it would have to be Daniel Pendleton. He had broad shoulders, a flat belly, and slim hips, all of which were shown off to perfection tonight in a well-tailored navy suit. His dark brown hair had just a hint of a wave, and the few lines on his forehead and around his eyes added maturity to a handsome face.

It was more than how he looked, though, she admitted. It was the quiet confidence he emanated. Everything about the way he walked and talked said, *Don't worry. I can take care of it.* Sara had to take only a baby step farther in her mind to wonder how a man like Daniel took care of a woman.

No.

Daniel Pendleton was in the prime of his life, a good man, Sara reminded herself, and she was convinced that it was her curse to ruin good men.

She shrugged. "I just don't think—"

"C'mon." He took her hand, lacing his fingers through hers, and tugged. "It's just a dance. I'm not gonna bite you."

Before she knew it, one of his large hands wrapped around her waist, the other firmly held her hand, and Sara was fighting a topsy-turvy sensation while she stared at the knot in Daniel's maroon club tie. She was suddenly acutely aware of her femininity in a way she hadn't in years.

And it felt entirely too good.

The texture of his hands lured her attention. A working-man's hands. She'd always been held by men with smooth, white-collar hands. Daniel's palms were callused, his fingers blunt, and Sara got the distinct impression that he was very selective about how he used his hands to convey strength and gentleness.

"What's wrong with my hand?"

Sara jerked her gaze up to his. "Nothing." Seeing the disbelief in his eyes, she searched for something to say. "It looks like it healed well."

"Yeah." He flexed his fingers around hers. "I lost my fingerprints in that fire, though. Now I could take up a life of crime and no one would be able to catch me."

Sara shook her head. "They'd remember your eyes. Besides, you're a good guy, the head of the clan, a pillar of the community. Your sense of integrity wouldn't let you do anything too bad."

His gaze held hers. "Even good men have their weaknesses, Sara."

Her stomach took a dip. She didn't expect this, not from Daniel.

He nudged her away from a couple who kept bumping into them. "Where did you spend Thanksgiving? Carly said she tried to rope you into coming to our celebration."

Despite Carly's repeated invitation, Sara drew the line at holiday get-togethers. Although she had a secret yearning to be part of a real family, she would have felt out of place. "Chattanooga."

He nodded. "You used to live there?"

"Yes." He seemed to be waiting for her to continue, so she reluctantly expounded. "I've helped serve food at the homeless shelter for the past three years. I guess it's become a tradition." Lord knew she didn't have many other holiday traditions.

"Oh."

Just a trace of skepticism oozed from that single word. Sara puzzled over his tone, searching his features . . . until she remembered what Daniel had said to her in that heated moment right before his soup had met his lap. A lick of anger spiked her pulse. "You don't sound like you believe me."

He hesitated, his brow furrowing. "Well, no . . ."

Sara could have kicked herself for allowing herself to get into this situation. She'd always made a point of avoiding Daniel. He thought she needed lessons in proper moral behavior. The crushing point of it was that there'd been a time when he wouldn't have been far off the mark.

Not anymore, dammit!

Fighting a sudden deluge of emotions, Sara stiffened, and tightened her grip on his shoulder. "What did you expect? That I entertained a few University of Tennessee fraternity houses?"

He shook his head. "I never—"

"You might as well have. I know what you think of me, Daniel. You made it very clear. You said you thought I was leading your precious baby sister down the path to ruin." Sara pulled her hands away from him. "If Carly coerced you into dancing with me, let me make myself clear. It isn't necessary. I'd just as soon you keep your distance."

Spinning away from him, Sara headed toward the galley. She'd just reached the hall when her hand was snagged, jerking her to a stop. She knew before turning who was in possession of her hand.

Daniel tugged her around. "Do you always jump to conclusions on the basis of one word?"

Sara pulled fruitlessly, glaring at him. "I *know* what you said about me being a bad influence."

"That was a long time ago, and it caught me off guard when Carly sent you to help me with my lunch after I'd burned my hands."

Not mollified, Sara pursed her lips. "You didn't have to insult me."

"You didn't have to dump the soup in my lap either."

Sara finally jerked her hand free. "I did not dump it in your lap. You were waving your arms like a madman."

His eyes went dark, and the suggestion of a

grin tugged at his mouth. "Guess being a madman should disqualify me from pillar-of-the-community status. So, how do you feel about having dinner with a fallen man?"

Sara blinked, feeling the currents between them shift yet again. "No," she said instinctively. The word came easily to her. "You're doing this because Carly put you up to it and—"

He pressed his index finger over her mouth, stopping her breath with that one touch. "Carly doesn't have anything to do with this." He paused only a second, his expression deadly serious. "I'm asking you for me."

Sara's stomach twisted into a knot, and she prayed for him to remove his finger.

He did, pulling his hand away, studying her. "What do you say?"

Sara barely held in a sigh of relief. "I say you're crazy."

Daniel frowned. Her response wasn't what he'd hoped, but Daniel had always favored the direct approach. It was the same way he approached most things in life. Lengthy deliberation followed by swift action. "Sara—"

"Sara." Carly's voice rang out.

She began backing away. "It's Carly. Gotta go." She gave a too-cheery smile. "Good-bye."

She was a vanishing blur of brown hair, black velvet, and fast-moving shapely legs. At a much slower pace Daniel went back to the main deck, realizing there was quite a bit he didn't know about Sara.

His brother Troy strolled up to him. "You ready to go?"

Daniel looked over the whole room, his gaze catching on the woman who'd occupied too much of his mind lately. Fresh determination surged through him. "Not yet. You might want to ride home with Jarod." He filched a single red rose from one of the many bouquets around the room, still keeping her in his sight. "I'll be late tonight."

I shouldn't have worn red.

Sara berated herself a dozen times as she pushed through the door of her two-bedroom home. On the way to her bedroom, she tossed her sensible black wool coat and leather purse onto the chintz floral sofa, kicked off her flat patent-leather shoes, and started working on the zipper to her demure black velvet dress.

She shimmied out of the dress, threw it on the bed, and pushed down her stockings and garter belt. Then she stood in her darkened bedroom wearing nothing but her sinful red silk slip.

She shouldn't have worn red.

Men seemed to sense it. She was convinced they had some kind of sonar when it came to detecting her past. No matter how prim the outer layer was, they seemed to sense the sensual Sara underneath it all, the Sara who enjoyed all kinds of pleasures, from the sensation of velvet, silk, sun, and water on her bare skin to the flavors of a succulent rare steak; fresh, yeasty bread; and strawberries dipped in rich, dark chocolate. The Sara who hid over a dozen bottles of perfume underneath her sink and had trouble deciding which to wear because she liked them all.

Sara pushed back the hair from her face in frustration. Even now, at the age of twenty-seven, she fought a constant battle with herself, torn somewhere between being the quiet, reserved woman who garnered the respect of the community and the sensual one she hid in the privacy of her home. The sensual one had been known to get her into trouble.

A stab of pain cut through her as she remembered the senator. He'd been such a nice, decent middle-aged man, but so lonely since his wife had been ill. Sara had been his receptionist. Her first job at eighteen, and she'd been thrilled and scared. It all began quite innocently with her working late nights, then having coffee with the senator and other staff at an all-night diner. He'd been like a father figure to her, and God knew she'd never had a father in her life.

When her apartment building had been destroyed in a fire, the senator found a place for her to live. It had been easier to say yes than no, easier to accept the affection she craved. He gave her a single red rose the day she moved in, and one yes led to another and another and . . .

One year later the press found out, and the nice senator blew his brains out.

Sara's mind seemed bent on punishing her tonight. The thought of her deceased husband loomed over her like a dark shadow, and still more guilt flooded her. When he'd learned about her past, he'd hated her for it. When he'd died in an automobile accident, he was still hating her.

Sara shuddered at the memories. Sinking down on her bed, she wrapped her arms around herself. She didn't want to turn on the light. She didn't want to see herself in the mirror. She needed to let the guilt and shame pass.

It would have been comforting to have a man hold her during that painful moment. An image of Daniel Pendleton with the strong, gentle hands and broad shoulders seeped through her mind like mist.

Sara impatiently shook it off and rose from the bed to turn on the light. She was lifting the hem of her slip to strip it off when her doorbell rang. She glanced at her brass alarm clock and frowned. Twelve-thirty. Who in the world could it be at this hour?

Snatching the ankle-length kimono from the hook on the back of her closet door, she wrapped it around herself, marched to her front door, and looked through the peephole.

Daniel Pendleton. Her heart gave a tiny, involuntary flutter.

She opened the door, saying the first thing that came to mind. "Is something wrong with Carly?"

"No." Daniel looked into Sara's wary eyes and immediately knew he'd have to temper the Romeo bit. She looked small and vulnerable and mussed in a thoroughly inviting way, but she also looked distrustful. He shoved the rosebud into his pocket and stepped through the doorway. "Mind if I come in?"

"Well—"

"I wanted to make sure you got home okay." He paused, sweeping the living room with a curious glance. His first impressions were of femininity, comfort, and privacy. Puffy curtains and pastel miniblinds covered the windows. On the mantel he noticed a lot of candles and a stuffed teddy bear wearing a floppy hat and lace dress. One end table held a best-selling novel, a few women's magazines, and a bottle of nail polish. An image flashed through his mind of Sara wearing the red silk slip as she painted her nails and blew them dry. He could almost feel the warmth of her breath, and just the thought of it made him tug at his starched collar.

Her coat and purse had been thrown carelessly on the floral sofa, which, in Daniel's opinion, held too many little pillows and was too small for sleeping. But he could imagine ditching those little pillows, easing Sara into his lap, and kissing her until they were both ready for bed.

He'd trade the lower forty for a peek at her bedroom.

"I'm fine," Sara said.

His gaze automatically went to her. "And we never finished our conversation."

Sara looked at him blankly.

Daniel's mouth lifted in a slow grin. "Dinner."

Uneasy, Sara picked up her coat and hung it in the closet, feeling Daniel's gaze track her every movement. He seemed to take up an enormous amount of space in her house. "I think it would be best if we didn't."

"Why?"

She wished he hadn't asked that. "Because you're Carly's brother and she's my boss."

Propping himself against the sofa, he crossed his arms over his chest. "So?"

"So it could get awkward." She tried, surreptitiously, to kick her shoes under an end table. When Daniel's gaze slid to her feet and seemed to settle on her red toenails, Sara felt terribly self-conscious. It was one of her little eccentricities. She painted her toenails bright, flashy colors while she kept her fingernails trimmed and painted them neutral colors. She cleared her throat, wishing for steel-toed boots.

He stood and walked closer to her, setting off all her warning bells and whistles.

"Does that mean you don't want to?" he asked.

Sara swallowed. "I—" She searched for an honest but polite response and came up empty.

His eyes narrowed thoughtfully as if he truly wanted to understand. "You don't like the way I look?"

She shook her head, wishing desperately that she wasn't having this conversation. "No. That's not—"

His gaze swept her from head to toe. "You're not attracted to me?"

She felt her cheeks heat. "I didn't say that."

"You're still missing your husband?" His voice held sympathy, but no pity.

He gave her the perfect excuse, and Sara almost took the easy way out. "I miss him." She felt dishonest letting the statement sit between them. Sighing, she lifted her hand and briefly touched his arm. "But that's not why I don't go out."

Daniel's hand slid out and captured hers. "Then I don't understand."

Sara's pulse jumped. A strong, solid male hand held hers, and the simple act short-circuited her brain. How could she explain that she had a unique ability to ruin good men? His thumb caressed her knuckles, and the gesture seemed more intimate than it should have. Was it the late hour or the man?

She took a deep breath. "I'm not very good at male-female relationships," she admitted.

"Maybe you're just out of practice," he said, twining their fingers together one by one. His gaze hovered on her mouth, and Sara had the oddest sensation of being thoroughly kissed. She could almost feel his mouth, soft and mobile, on hers. He would slowly slide his tongue past her teeth and explore her vulnerable softness, then tease her into giving him what he wanted. Oh, yes, she'd bet Daniel Pendleton would know how to tease a woman.

She shook her head at the sudden heat rising in her body. She licked her burning lips and heard his quick intake of breath.

He squeezed her fingers, a silent reprimand for her involuntarily provocative gesture. His gaze rose to meet hers. "Practice makes perfect, Sara, and I think," he said in a low, rough voice, looking at her through hooded violet eyes, "you should practice on me."

TWO

A flicker of awareness darkened Sara's eyes, then her eyelashes lowered as if they were a silk curtain. Daniel felt her withdrawal before she moved away.

She whispered something under her breath. He couldn't make out the words, but her tone was that of a chiding reminder. Clutching the front of her robe, she shook her head. "It's so late. I appreciate"—she hesitated, leading him to believe she did *not* appreciate it—"your checking on me. It was kind of you. I'm getting up early tomorrow morning." She moved toward the door. "I bet you are too."

She put her hand on the doorknob, and Daniel experienced the urge to goad her into dropping the polite shield. She exhibited the dignity of a queen, and her will was far stronger than he'd anticipated.

He reluctantly admired her at the same time that he was stymied by her.

Shoving his hand into his pocket in frustration, he felt something sharp jab his finger. He jerked, grimacing. A thorn from that damn rose, he realized belatedly.

Most of his calculations about Sara had been off tonight. Cranky enough to use Sara's politeness against her, he walked toward her.

"I guess we'll have to figure out those dinner arrangements another time," he said, getting closer and closer, betting the clutching and unclutching of her hand meant that his nearness made her nervous. That was okay. Nervous was better than nothing.

She opened her mouth to refuse, he was certain, and Daniel covered her hand on the doorknob, stopping her cold.

Feeling both predatory and frustrated, he smiled. "You're going to Erin and Garth's wedding, aren't you?"

She hesitated. "Yes."

"Carly said your car's been a little temperamental, so I'll take you."

He bent his head toward her and watched another protest die on her lips. "See you next Saturday," he said, pushing the door open. He took one last glance at her before he left, and what he saw sent his blood pressure into the ozone. Her robe gaped slightly, and underneath that long robe sweet Sara

Kingston was wearing the wicked red slip from his dream.

"Is Sara off today?" Daniel asked his sister with forced nonchalance.

Carly shook her head. "No. She's gone to the post office. She'll probably be back in a few minutes." Carly riffled through the papers on the top of her desk, obviously looking for something. "Why do you want to know?"

Daniel shrugged. "No reason. When I made sure she got home from the party the other night, she seemed a little edgy."

Carly frowned. "Edgy? I wondered about that. She's been dropping things lately."

His interest perked up. "Dropping things?"

"Yeah. Like on the floor." She pulled a letter from the pile and smiled. "There it is." She turned her attention toward Daniel. "I noticed you danced with her at the party."

Baby sister didn't miss a thing. "You said you wished I would act nicer to her."

Suspicion glinted in her eyes. "You didn't make any lewd propositions, did you?"

Daniel didn't consider them lewd. He lifted his hands in innocence. "Me?"

Carly wasn't totally convinced. "I'd like you to bear in mind that I couldn't replace her if she quit. She's competent enough to run this business without me. I told you about how her husband died, and since you know what a good friend she's been to me," she said meaningfully, "I hope you will be careful with her. She's more tender-hearted than she appears."

"I'm always careful," Daniel muttered, feeling a sharp jab of irritation. Since he was the oldest, he'd always had to be careful. Every once in a while he'd like to indulge himself and do something irresponsible, disreputable, and enjoyable, but he always managed to restrain himself. Lately that restraint was wearing thin.

As for Sara's heart, he had no desire to claim it. He wanted her body. And he just wanted to *borrow* it until he got her out of his system. It had become a matter of survival, and it would be his greatest pleasure to make sure Sara got as much out of their affair as he did. "There's nothing for you to worry about."

A knock sounded at the door. "Carly?"

"Come in," Carly called.

Sara pushed open the door, holding a stack of papers. "I need to clarify something on this contract with—" She saw Daniel and promptly dropped the papers.

"Oh my." Distressed, Sara dropped to her knees. She wasn't a fumbler. She made it a point not to fumble, trip, or fidget. It was all part of the cool, competent image she worked hard to project. That cool, competent image covered a boatload of vulnerability and self-doubt. The senator had helped her acquire a poise that lifted her beyond her seedy background. But the last few days, to her chagrin, she'd been a total klutz, all because of Daniel Pendleton.

Suddenly Daniel was beside her on the floor, collecting the papers. "Here, let me help you."

"No. That's okay." Past caring that the papers were out of order, she gathered them together in her hands as quickly as possible. "I think I've got them now."

She stood; Daniel followed. She could feel his gaze on her, and an awkward silence hummed between them.

Out of the corner of her eye she saw him shove his hands into his pockets. She wondered what that gesture meant. She'd once read an article about how body language often told the truth more than a person's words did.

"Since I was in town today," Daniel ventured, "I was wondering if either of you ladies would like to have lunch with me. I thought I'd try one of those places on the wharf."

Carly sighed, shaking her head. "Count me out." She pointed toward the desk. "All you have to do is take a look at my desk."

Relieved that Carly had paved the way so nicely

for her, Sara shrugged. "I brought a sandwich to eat at my desk, so . . ."

Carly looked contrite. "Sara, don't feel like you've got to miss lunch just because I'm working. You've stayed late every night this week."

Sara shook her head. "But—"

"I'm beginning to feel like Simon Legree and Scrooge all rolled into one. Please. Appease my guilt and go."

Feeling cornered, Sara glanced at Daniel, then back at Carly. "Are you sure? I'm so distracted with these contracts, I'm sure I'll be rotten company."

"I'm sure," Carly said.

Daniel hitched one dark eyebrow in amusement. Sara knew he could tell she was trying to get out of it. "I'm sure too," he said in a low, taunting voice.

And he was, Sara thought. Daniel Pendleton was always insufferably sure of himself. It was one more reason for her not to like him. "I'll get my coat," she said reluctantly, deciding to order something that could be eaten quickly.

To her dismay they ended up at the Cimarron Rose, where barbecued baby back ribs, onion-ring loaves, and gooey cinnamon rolls were the order of the day.

"A salad," she said firmly.

"Anything else?" the waitress asked.

"No. Just a salad."

Daniel frowned for a moment, then gave his order—an entire rack of those baby back ribs along with crab legs and a baked potato.

Sara reconsidered her choice. There was no reason to deprive herself of some of her favorite foods just because she was eating with Daniel. It wasn't as if they were sharing a candlelight dinner for two in the privacy of her home. That thought gave her a jolt.

The waitress sent Daniel a broad smile and started to leave.

"I've changed my mind," Sara said quickly, not meeting Daniel's gaze. "I'd like an onion-ring loaf, a half rack of baby back ribs, western-style sauce, and a baked potato." She closed the menu. "Please."

"Sure you don't want crab legs?" Daniel asked after the waitress left. He wore a subtle, teasing grin.

"No." Sara chewed her lip to keep from smiling back at him, but failed. "If I eat any more, you'll have to wheel me out of here in a cart."

Daniel's gaze fell over her in assessment. "I wouldn't need a cart to carry you even if you tripled your order. Not with your weight."

"You have no idea what my weight is," Sara said, turning the subject away from the notion of him "carrying" her.

"Bet I could guess."

The way he said it caused a tickling sensation in

her stomach. She usually squashed this kind of flirty conversation. It was too personal, and she needed to keep her distance. But something about him, the I-dare-you-lady expression, made her want to accept the little challenge. "Okay. Winner gets the onion-ring loaf."

His eyes widened. "High stakes. How close do I have to get?"

Sara stared at him, feeling her pulse leap. *Close.*

"In pounds," he clarified.

Her mind going blank with relief, she pulled a figure out of nowhere. "*Two* pounds."

"Oooh. That's tough." He shook his head. "I'll give it a try."

That was when Sara realized this conversation had been a huge error. Daniel's gaze measured her neck, and she felt the warmth of it as if his hands gently touched her skin. He studied the width of her shoulders down her white silk blouse to her elbows. Then she watched the motion of his eyes as they moved to the bow that rested against her throat.

Sara's breath hung suspended while, ever so slowly, that violet gaze lowered to assess her breasts. Beyond her lacy bra his gaze caressed like fingers, cupping the weight of her, testing her softness. Sara felt a stinging arousal shoot straight to her nipples. Her face flamed with heat, and she nearly grabbed a napkin to hide herself.

Daniel stared straight at the center of her swollen breasts.

Sara bit her lip. Unable to stand his scrutiny any longer, she crossed her arms. "Time's—"

"One hundred and seventeen pounds," he said in a rough voice, reaching for his water glass. "One nineteen after you've just gotten out of a shower and you're soaking wet."

He sounded as if that last idea appealed to him. How had this discussion gotten so intimate? "How on earth did you guess?" she choked out.

He gave a chuckle and shook his head. "You wouldn't like my answer."

"Why?"

"Because my expertise comes from hauling bags of feed and sizing up livestock."

"So," Sara said, knowing she should be insulted, but smothering laughter instead, "as a point of reference for guessing my weight, you used cows and horses."

Daniel grinned. "You're exaggerating. More like pigs and goats."

This time Sara laughed. She couldn't help it.

The waitress delivered the food, and during the course of the meal Sara had a tough time keeping up her guard. It was difficult to remain prim and proper when you were up to your elbows in barbecue sauce.

"Is your schedule busy in the winter?"

Daniel shrugged. "It's nothing like spring or summer, but there always seems to be enough to do. Old Mr. Johnson had a dead tree he wanted cut into firewood, so I took care of that yesterday. I'm in charge of the emergency services for Beulah County. I twist arms and try to get the mayor to spend more money."

Nothing he told her surprised her. People depended on Daniel, and he came through. "And now there's the wedding for your brother and Erin. They both seem very happy," Sara said.

Daniel nodded. "He worships the ground Erin walks on."

"What do you think of that?"

Daniel paused for a moment, thinking. "She's done something for him no one else has. He's different now. He even laughs more."

"You sound surprised," Sara said, wiping her fingers.

"I guess I am. Garth's always been the wild one. It's as if he's been looking for something for a long time, and he finally found it. I always worried that he wouldn't."

Sara smiled. "Do I hear the big brother talking?"

Daniel felt a twist of irony at the question. He hadn't always enjoyed the role of big brother. "Yeah," he admitted reluctantly. "What about you? Do you have any brothers or sisters?"

"Not that I know of," Sara said dryly.

He frowned, thinking that was an odd response. "Does that mean you might have some, or you just don't know who they are?"

Sara debated sharing any of her background with Daniel. It wasn't something she was proud of. She rarely discussed her past. Then again, it would show the contrast in their upbringing. Maybe Daniel would draw the logical conclusion that they weren't suited, and his interest would wane. The thought brought relief and a certain, unwelcome uneasiness.

Pushing away the uneasiness, Sara went ahead. "I didn't have the same kind of family life you did—and still have."

Daniel shrugged. "Most people don't have six brothers and one sister."

"No. I mean, my mother was what we now call a single parent."

Continuing to study her, he took a sip of beer. "Like Erin," he said.

"Not quite." What an understatement. Erin Lindsey loved her son. She would lay down her life before she gave up her child. Sara hesitated, feeling her appetite wane. "My mother didn't have time to care for a child. She was busy with other things."

"Like?"

"Men."

Daniel was raising his glass to his mouth but stopped mid-movement. There was a wealth of emotion in that one word—*men*. He noticed that she'd tensed up again, and he wondered who Sara blamed, her mother or the men. He saw the turbulence in her eyes and felt a corresponding ripple within him. "Bet that was tough."

Sara searched his features, expecting to see disdain or disapproval. She found neither. "It was when I lived with her." Unpleasant memories swam from the back of her mind. "And sometimes when I didn't."

"You lived with other relatives sometimes?"

She shook her head. The other relatives hadn't wanted anything to do with her. Bad breeding, they'd said. And, in some ways, she thought, feeling a twist in her stomach, they'd been right. She blinked away the thoughts. "Foster homes."

"What about your dad?"

Sara stared at the table. She wished she'd kept her mouth shut. Saying it out loud only made it worse. "I've never met him."

A hint of vulnerability showed in her voice. It grabbed at his gut and pulled. She wasn't whining or cursing, yet, despite her composure, a little hurt and shame came through. He wasn't immune to it. Daniel cleared his throat. "I'm sorry."

Surprised, Sara looked up, but instead of the censure she'd expected, she found empathy. His simple words touched a vulnerable place inside her, one she kept hidden. She didn't know what to say.

"It's disappointing when your parents don't turn out the way you think they should." He rubbed the condensation on his glass. "It's the kind of disappointment that can stick with you a long time even if you don't want it to."

He spoke as if he had some experience with the same kind of disappointment, she thought. It made him seem more human to her, more likable, and made her feel a tenuous connection with him. It also made her wonder what his disappointments were. She toyed with asking him until she saw the expression on his face change from intent to teasing.

As if he realized the serious tone of their discussion had gone on long enough, he whispered to her in a conspiratorial tone, "Speaking of things that stick with you, we'd better eat these ribs before they get cold. Carly will give me hell if I don't make sure you get fed. She's scared you're gonna realize your true potential and leave her flat."

Sara stared at him, and a smile unfurled on her lips. "Why in the world would she think I'm going to leave her?"

"She said you can run *Matilda's Dream* without her."

A flush of pleasure stole over her, overshadowing their previous discussion. "I have no intention of leaving—"

Daniel gave her plate a meaningful glance. "Then do me a favor and eat."

Sara saw through his obvious maneuver to bring a happier mood to the meal. She should have been immune to his exaggeration, but, Lord help her, it felt great to have a good man teasing her. She saw the tempered desire in his eyes and felt adrenaline rush through her. Sara shook her head in skepticism at her roller-coaster feelings and took a bite of rib. "If you were so concerned about feeding me, then why did you eat my onion loaf?"

With a completely straight face he said, "I won that onion loaf by guessing your weight. It was my duty to eat it."

Sara laughed. "Duty!"

"When you're the oldest of eight, you learn very quickly that some duties are more desirable than others."

"You must have been a trial for your parents."

"According to my mother, I was perfect."

Sara rolled her eyes and delicately licked one of her fingers. "Spoken like a first child."

Daniel watched, fascinated by the sensuality of the small movement. Throughout the meal he'd gotten the impression that occasionally Sara indulged herself, and the way she indulged herself with food was sexy. She didn't mind the messiness. As a matter of fact she seemed to revel in it.

She took another bite of ribs and slowly ran the

slick, pink tip of her tongue over her upper lip.

Daniel's gut tightened.

Sara stopped. "Is something wrong?"

Yes, Daniel thought. Something was wrong. He wished they were alone so that he could taste that erotic mouth of hers and find out if she was as sweet and spicy as he suspected. He found himself wishing for a lot of things when he was around her. Sara made him feel . . . deprived. He cleared his throat. "You missed a little sauce on the left."

Sara lifted her napkin and wiped her mouth. "Here?"

He shook his head. "No." Giving in to his need, he leaned forward and touched her mouth with his thumb.

Sara went completely still. His gaze, she noted, was fixed with mesmerizing intent on her mouth, as if he couldn't have torn his attention from her if he'd wanted to. He rubbed gently and should have moved away then. Instead his thumb moved from one side of her mouth and back.

Sara held her breath.

Daniel lifted his gaze to meet hers and pressed his thumb into the center of her lips.

A kiss.

She felt it and instinctively pursed her mouth against him.

His eyes flared, and he pressed a little farther,

his thumb invading the soft moistness of her inner lips.

Surprised by his unexpected boldness, Sara felt a sensual twisting deep inside her coiling tighter and tighter. Masculine hunger was there on his face, something she hadn't expected from Daniel. What she'd expected even less was her own overwhelming fascination with him. Shocking, intimate images floated through her mind.

Sara closed her eyes against them. She moved to dampen her suddenly dry lips and instead tasted his flesh.

Daniel swore.

Mortified, Sara instantly pulled back, but the tension between them held her like a chain. "I'm sorry," she whispered, staring and shaking her head. "I don't know—"

"Hey, Daniel," a male voice called, "we've been looking all over for you. I thought you were gonna eat lunch with Carly."

Troy stopped at the table.

Sara jerked her gaze from Daniel and cleared her throat. She took a deep breath and looked up to see not only Troy but also Jarod. She forced a smile. "Hi."

Troy and Jarod greeted her, then Troy slid beside Daniel, and Jarod sat beside her.

"I thought you two were doing maintenance on the machinery this morning," Daniel said.

Troy shrugged. "We needed a part." He shot Sara a coy glance. "We thought we'd join you and Carly for lunch."

An uncomfortable silence followed, and Sara felt the same underlying uneasiness she always felt when she was with the Pendleton brothers. The problem was that since they had a shared history, they knew all the inside family jokes, the pecking order, and what subjects were taboo. They knew, and she didn't, which made her feel more like an outsider than ever.

Daniel nearly groaned. "Carly was busy, like you're supposed to be."

"We needed that part and . . ."

"Is the Christmas season keeping you and Carly busy with *Matilda's Dream?*" Jarod asked Sara, pulling her attention away from Troy and Daniel.

She nodded. "Christmas and end-of-the-year reports." Growing more uncomfortable with each passing moment, she glanced at her watch. "Oh my! Look at the time. I need to get back."

"I can walk you," Jarod offered.

Anger pulsed through Daniel. He nearly pounded his fist on the table. After all his careful planning he'd lost complete control of this situation. Troy was starting to jaw about being hungry, and heaven help him, it looked as if Jarod was moving in on Sara.

"*I'll* walk her," Daniel announced in a voice that brooked no argument.

"Oh, no." Sara stood. "You can't leave your brothers."

"Why not?"

She blinked. "Well, they just got here, and . . ." She shrugged and managed a strained smile. "And now you can discuss whatever it is that brothers talk about. Thank you for lunch." She waved a hand, encompassing all of them. "I'll see you at the wedding."

Troy and Jarod murmured their agreement.

Daniel called after Sara. "I'll pick you up at two o'clock."

He watched Sara move her head in a gesture that could have meant yes or no.

"You're finally making your move," Troy piped in with a smirk on his face.

At that moment Daniel would have traded his name to be an only child. Furious with his lack of privacy, he tried to lay some ground rules. First things first. He turned to Jarod. "Cut the moves on Sara."

Jarod lifted his hands in surprise. "Hey, I was just trying to put her at ease."

Daniel frowned. "Well, don't try so hard. And you," he said, turning to Troy. "If you ever horn in again when I'm with her, I swear I'll—"

"Horn in!" Troy lowered his voice. "Does that mean you were getting anywhere with her?"

Daniel hesitated, remembering how she'd kissed

his thumb. For a little slice of time her eyes had gone soft and hazy.

Then he recalled how quickly she'd left. If he were going to answer Troy, he supposed he'd have to say yes and no. He decided, though, that he wanted his relationship with Sara kept private. Because he felt a strong protectiveness toward her. And because there was no way he could articulate what he felt for her. It was overwhelming and disturbing.

He looked at Troy and Jarod, and for the first time in his life he made a demand that had nothing to do with the farm or the family and everything to do with himself. "Leave it alone. Just leave it alone."

THREE

Sara watched Garth take Erin in his arms for a long and thorough kiss. Several seconds passed, and Troy started making whooping noises. Another brother, Brick, let out a loud whistle. Pretty soon most of the wedding guests were applauding. The couple finally pulled apart. Erin's face was flushed with pleasure, Garth's expression was tinged with awe, and the look they exchanged was so intimate that Sara had to turn away.

She glanced at Daniel to find him looking at her. Her stomach dipped.

You don't belong here, Sara Jean.

I know. I know. But I can wish, can't I? Wishing won't hurt anyone.

You can wish all you want to, but you'll never be like these people. You're too much like—

Sara mentally cut off her mother's voice. She

heard it only when she was feeling vulnerable, like today. The simple ceremony had made Sara feel a little weepy. It reminded her that she didn't share a close, loving relationship with anyone on this planet. The reminder hurt.

"Are you okay?" Carly asked, concern etched on her face.

Sara shook off her depressed mood and smiled. "Fine. Erin looks beautiful."

Carly sighed. "She does. But I'd probably look that radiant, too, if I were going to Martinique."

Overhearing that last comment, Carly's husband, Russ, came up from behind and pulled her against him. He tossed Sara a wink. "We can have our own little island in the sun tonight in the Jacuzzi."

Carly laughed. "Have you forgotten that we're looking after Luke while Erin and Garth are on their honeymoon?"

Russ shook his head. "He'll be so tired after all the activity today." He gave them both a broad grin, kissed Carly, then backed away to answer someone's greeting.

Carly rolled her eyes, but Sara could tell she was delighted with her husband.

"So," said Carly, pulling her attention from Russ. "How's everything progressing with Daniel? I hear he nearly beat up Jarod and Troy for interrupting your lunch the other day."

Sara blinked at the change in subject, then shook her head. "Daniel and I aren't progressing anywhere because we're not well suited for each other. I told you that before."

"That was before he decided to go after you."

Sara's pulse accelerated. "He'll change his mind."

Carly looked at Sara with sympathy. "How long have you been suffering from delusions? Get ready for the chase of your life." She made a tsking sound. "You're so nice and innocent. Just don't let him push you into doing anything you don't want to."

Russ reappeared and snagged Carly's wrist. "You're not meddling, are you?"

Carly innocently batted her eyes at him. "Not me." Then she ducked her head and whispered to Sara, "One more warning: When Daniel wants something, he can have the sensitivity of a Mack truck."

Frustrated, Sara shook her head. "But I—"

"Are you ready for the reception?" Daniel asked from beside her. He placed his hand on her back and watched her take a deep breath. There was turbulence in her green-gray eyes. He wondered what she and Carly had been talking about. He wondered a lot about Sara Kingston. Lately he'd been wondering what her lips would feel like pressed to his. And he decided that tonight he would find out.

❖━━━━━━━━━━❖

"Thanks for the ride," Sara said, reaching for her key.

"No problem," Daniel said. She was going to try to leave him on the porch. He knew it. "Mind if I have a cup of coffee?"

Sara jerked her head up to look at him. He could hear his mother's voice scolding him: *Pushy, pushy, pushy. Wait until you're invited.* Tough. At this rate, if he waited for an invitation from Sara, he'd never get past the front door, let alone into her bed.

Her ever-present politeness warred with a desire to kick him out. He could read it on her face. "Of course," Sara finally said, then pushed open the door. "Come on in."

She started to take off her coat and Daniel helped her with it. He caught a whiff of her sweet and spicy perfume. "You smell great."

"It's new, and I probably shouldn't have gotten it," she said, remembering how the romantic fragrance had captivated her at the cosmetic counter just the other day. "I have all these bottles under my sink, but I love perfume and I just can't seem to resist . . ." Her voice stalled when he touched her.

Under the guise of a casual gesture, Daniel lifted her hair behind her shoulder and played with a silky brown strand. "I'm glad you didn't resist. Did you know your hair even smells like it?"

Sara swallowed hard. "Bath gel and shampoo came with it."

Daniel felt his temperature rise. "So you smell like this all . . ." His imagination flashed a vivid picture of Sara, wet, scented, and nude, in a bathtub.

"All over," she finished in a slightly husky voice. Then she cleared her throat. "About that coffee."

"Yeah."

Sara looked at him expectantly. "I, uh, need my hair."

Still reluctant to let go, he grinned and tangled his fingers deeper into her hair. "So do I."

"Are you flirting with me?"

"I'm trying." His grin grew. "Is it working?"

Too well. Her pulse racing, she tamped down the urge to rest her head in his big hand. Instead she tried to distract him. "I have some hot chocolate."

"And marshmallows?"

A little boy when it came to food, she concluded. Darn if that didn't make her like him more. "Yes."

He loosened his fingers and leaned closer. "You didn't answer my question."

Still entangled in his gaze, Sara gave a quick shake of her head and backed away. "I'm not going to."

For several moments he looked at her hungrily. "Guess I'll have to keep trying, Miss Sara."

Distressed, she lifted a hand. "Please don't."

"Why?"

She bit her lip and knitted her fingers together. "We've already talked about this."

Daniel nodded. "I know. First you said I should leave you alone because of Carly. Then you said you didn't think you were good at male-female relationships." He crossed his arms over his chest and leaned against the wall. "So what is it tonight?"

"You're not making this easy for me."

"And you're not making it easy for me either."

She refused to let his persistence wear her down. "Daniel, you're a good man. And I'm not"—she groped for the proper words—"I'm not good for good men. I ruin them."

He gave a burst of laughter. "You're nuts," he said. "You're sexy as hell. But you're nuts. You couldn't ruin a peapod."

She sucked in a harsh breath. "How about a senator?"

His laughter faltered. "What?"

She shook her head. There were some things she simply couldn't discuss, even for the sake of Daniel Pendleton. "I don't want to go into it, so just trust me. Two men, two good men, lost everything because of their relationships with me. I don't want the same thing to happen to you."

Daniel scratched his head. "Now, let me get this straight. You think you're responsible for the downfall of these two men." He waved his hand. "That it's somehow related to you."

"Definitely," Sara said in a solemn voice.

"And," he continued, "you think that if you get involved with me, you'll ruin my life."

Sara nodded.

He rolled his eyes and tugged his tie loose. "I gotta tell you, Sara. That's the biggest bunch of bull I've heard in my life. And with Troy as my brother, I've heard a hell of a lot."

Sara stiffened. "I'm sorry if you don't believe it, but it's true." She turned and headed for the kitchen.

Daniel followed after her. "You really expect me to believe that you lure good men down the road to perdition? How did you do it, Sara? Did you put a magic potion in their hot chocolate? Did you sprinkle fairy dust on them when they slept? How did you do it?"

She gritted her teeth together, took the milk from the refrigerator, and poured it into a pan. "It's a little more basic than that."

Completely baffled, he shook his head. "Then it must be one of the top three ways to a man's heart—money, food, or—"

Sara whipped around, her eyes shooting off enough sparks to set the kitchen on fire. "Sex."

Daniel fell silent. He cleared his throat, never easing his gaze from hers. "You want to explain that?"

Sara sent up a silent prayer for deliverance from men with violet eyes, broad shoulders, and too many questions. "I thought it was self-explanatory." The milk began to simmer, and she turned away to reach for the cocoa.

In an instant he was behind her, staying her arm and turning off the burner. "The chocolate can wait. You can't just say something like that and go on like you're discussing the weather."

Oh, Lord, he was going to make her say it. He was the kind of man to expect complete honesty, and something about him made her want to deliver what he expected. Maybe if she tried to explain it, she told herself, he would understand and stop this insanity.

Where were the words? Sighing, Sara stared at the clock on the stove. The second hand made jerky little movements that seemed to echo the beat of her heart. "They said I was good at it. The first man who"—she swallowed—"who taught me said I seemed to have a natural propensity for it. He told me," she continued with irony, "that I had a *talent* for making a man hot. Back then I was so stupid, I thought he was paying me a compliment." She took a deep breath. "My husband concurred."

She felt a ripping sensation inside her. Exposing herself this way left her raw and vulnerable. Covering it as best as she could with a tight smile, she turned. "So here I am with my little bag of feminine tricks and talent." It would have been more accurate to say that here she was with all her feminine need and unquenched desire, but she wouldn't say it.

She turned toward Daniel and made herself look at him, determined to do the right thing. "You tempt me, Daniel Pendleton. Yes," she said, seeing the sensual recognition in his gaze, "you make me think about what I'm missing. You make me think about what it's like to hold and be held. To spend a night so lost in pleasure that night turns to day and day turns to night." She bit her lip, appalled at all she'd revealed, horrified at what she'd admitted. She shook her head. "But you're a good man. And I'm not going to ruin any more good men. I'm not going to ruin you."

Several seconds passed in thoughtful silence. Daniel watched Sara and felt even more determined to have her. That she wanted to protect him was precious; ludicrous, but precious. That she thought he was an angel was a problem. "What if I'm not all that good?"

Tension eased from Sara at his response. After her desperate confession, she'd expected something more condemning. "If being responsible were a crime, you'd get life in prison for it."

"Don't rub it in." He pushed his hands into his pockets and turned away in frustration. "Do you have any idea what it's like being the oldest of eight? My father nearly lost it after my mother died. That was right around driving age for me. You know, the time when guys play on the football team, take the girls out on Saturday night, and see how far they'll let you go in the backseat. Well, if you're busy trying to cover your old man's butt, then there's no time for that stuff. Carly was little, and when she wasn't crying, she was stuttering. Garth was always getting into trouble. I would have been raising a little hell myself, but—"

Sara began to understand. "But you were too busy raising a family." She sighed. "Did you ever get to choose, to do what you wanted?"

He slowly turned and met her gaze. "Not until now."

Sara's stomach tightened. "See," she said in a softly accusing tone. "I told you you're a good man."

Daniel shook his head. "I didn't want to do the right things. I was angry and frustrated. I resented all that responsibility."

She felt an overwhelming need to convince him of his worth. It disturbed her that he didn't seem to realize it. It made her wonder why his family had been so blind. "That's not the point. You did what you had to, anyway." She stepped forward, touching his arm when he looked skeptical. "You did your best. That's what separates the good men from"—she smiled—"the not-so-good men."

He took her hand and twined his fingers through hers. "That still leaves me with the same problem. I never got to sow my oats. Never got to go parking on a Saturday night. I'm not without experience," he confessed. "But I've always been discreet and respectable." A dangerous light came into his eyes. Tugging her closer, he lifted her hand to his cheek. "Even if it ruins him, Sara, every man needs to have one forbidden affair with a wild woman."

He moved her hand to his mouth and kissed it.

The warmth of his mouth kindled her nerve endings. Her heart beat unevenly. He darted his tongue out to taste the tender skin on the inside of her wrist, and Sara's breath was squeezed from her lungs.

"I can handle the risk, honey," he said in a low, husky voice. "Ruin me."

FOUR

"Oh, Daniel," Sara whispered in a shaky voice.

He watched the struggle play across her face. Her pupils dilated with arousal, and she bit her upper lip.

Her desire lit a fire in his gut, and he pulled her closer as he placed her hand behind his neck. Slowly he trailed his fingers down her other arm to her hand and lifted that one behind his neck also. All the while he looked deeply into her eyes. "You said I make you remember what it's like to hold and be held. Don't you want to do more than remember?"

Sara closed her eyes against the powerful attraction brewing between them. "This isn't fair. I told you—"

Her voice broke off when Daniel slid one of his hands to the small of her back and with his other hand tilted her chin. Her skin was soft and flushed beneath his touch. So tender, yet his body's reaction was strong and unmistakable. He rubbed his thumb over the velvet lushness of her bottom lip. Even the way her breath caught turned him on. "I've been wondering what it would be like to kiss you. Don't you ever wonder about me?"

Her eyes fluttered open, and she swallowed. "Of course I do," she murmured, her voice a husky reprimand.

Feeling the smallest rush of male triumph, he sifted his fingers through her silky hair and leaned closer until his lips were a whisper away from hers. He teased himself and her with the slight distance, and the wanting surged between them. "Don't you ever want to do more than wonder?"

Her breathing grew labored, but she didn't answer.

"No answer?" Too stubborn to say yes, he decided, but too aroused to pull away. His pulse bucked. God, she made him want her. "I want more than wondering."

He lowered his head and took her mouth. He absorbed the texture of Sara, her mouth soft and full against his, her body warm and feminine in his arms. Maybe it should have been enough, but it wasn't. She made him want more. He rubbed his tongue over her lips back and forth, until with a sigh that had his blood pressure zooming she opened.

She tasted like every forbidden delicacy he'd been denied. Sweet and dark like the richest of chocolate with the kick of premium champagne. For a moment he felt rough and awkward next to her delicate femininity. He wondered if he'd read her incorrectly. Maybe she didn't want him.

But then she was sliding her hands through his hair, caressing his mouth with hers, and she wasn't just warm anymore. She was hot.

Her tongue was a silken, teasing reminder of the pleasure exchanged between a woman and a man, and he had to curb his overwhelming instinct to thrust. His heart thudding like a jackhammer, he slowly pulled her against the ache she'd started. He hesitated, wondering if she'd back away.

Instead a layer of her inhibitions seemed to fall off, and if he didn't know better, he'd say she needed to be as close to him as he did to her. She stretched against him, her breasts pressing into his chest, so that he could feel her peaked nipples. The sensation made him want to tear off his shirt and her dress.

Then she gave him the most delightful shock of his life. She opened her thighs, nestled his erection between her legs, and gently swiveled against him.

Provocative and welcoming, the movement was all female to his male. Daniel thrust his tongue into her mouth at the same time that he rolled his lower body against her.

Sara moaned, clutching at his shoulders.

Something inside him snapped at the sound she made. He wrapped his hands around her buttocks and gently squeezed, then pulled her skirt up her hips until he felt a garter, the bare skin of her thigh, and the heat between her legs. Want, he was consumed with it. Want and need. She was a flash fire in his blood.

He tugged at her panties.

Sara ripped her mouth from his. "No! Oh God, no!" Her voice was a distressed whimper directed more to herself than to him. Her eyes wild and desperate, she pushed her skirt down and nearly tripped over her own feet as she backed away, wrapping her arms around herself.

Daniel's body pulsed with unappeased arousal. As if his body were locked into one mode, his hands remained outstretched toward Sara. To his horror they were trembling. He clenched his fists and shoved them into his pockets. The haze of his desire slowly cleared.

Embarrassed beyond belief, Sara covered her hot cheeks. "I'm sorry. I-I-" She swallowed, and shook her head. What had gotten into her? "I can't explain it. It's just been such a long time for me and—"

"Don't," Daniel interrupted. He held up a hand. "Just don't."

But Sara couldn't handle it. She felt guilty,

embarrassed, and, adding to her mortification, still aroused. "I don't know what came over me. I meant to pull away, but then your arms were around me and you kissed me and . . ." She shoved her hair behind her ears. "It felt—"

"Stop." Frustrated, Daniel roughly ran a hand through his own hair. He sighed. "I was all over you like a damn rutting buck. It's no wonder—"

"No!" Sara saw the look of bewilderment on Daniel's face, but she simply could not let him take responsibility for the way things had gotten out of control. Sure, he'd pushed a little, but it hadn't taken much for him to make her forget all her resolutions. "You didn't let me finish," she said in a much quieter voice, feeling her face heat in anticipation of her confession. She took a deep breath. "I was going to say that it felt good. More than good to be held and"—she allowed her gaze to slide away from his—"touched by you. I guess I kinda lost it."

"That makes two of us."

She glanced up, hearing the deep, sensual tone of his voice. She'd ruffled his dark hair with her fingers. His cheeks still held the dusky tint of arousal. His mouth was swollen, as she was sure hers was too. His tie had fallen to the floor, and the first few buttons of his shirt were undone. Oh, Lord, when had she done that?

The worst part was that his facial expression and

the way he stood all said he hadn't minded one bit that she'd kinda lost it. And he wouldn't mind if she kinda lost it again.

Her heart dipped. "It won't happen again."

He shifted his stance. "We're attracted to each other."

Her better judgment was returning. She moved away from him and put the cocoa back in the cabinet. They wouldn't be sharing a cup of hot chocolate. "I know, but it would be best if we didn't see each other."

"Seems stupid to me."

Sara paused, her back still to him. *Stupid?*

"I want you. You want me. We could spend some time together." He shrugged. "Or I can go home and think about you. And you can think about me. And we can be lonely."

Lonely. The word made something inside her twist painfully. She was well acquainted with the state of loneliness. She knew well the endless ways that a person could be lonely. She also knew that she'd handled loneliness before. It wasn't fun, but it kept her out of trouble. She turned. "You have your family."

A restlessness came into his eyes. "It's not the same thing, and you know it."

"We aren't even friends."

He went very still. "Do you want to be?"

Sara sighed. Did she want to be? Did it matter

what she wanted? Of course not. Unable to meet his gaze, she looked at the floor. "Earlier you said you can handle the risk." She lifted her shoulders. "Maybe you can." Biting her lip, she shook her head. "But I can't."

During the next few days Sara tried to blot out the memory of that scene. She tried to forget how wonderful it had felt to be held by Daniel Pendleton. She tried not to think about how he'd left. He hadn't argued or tried to cajole her into changing her mind. He'd just looked at her with those violet eyes that seared her soul, and then he'd left. Her cozy little house that had seemed crowded when he was in it suddenly felt empty and too quiet.

Her concentration was shot straight to hell in a handbasket. Even now Carly was talking, and Sara had missed the last half of the conversation. She gave herself a hard mental shake.

"So will you do it?" Carly asked.

"Do what?"

Carly rolled her eyes. "Sara, I'm beginning to think your mind has moved to the Great Beyond. That's the second time this week you've zoned out on me. What's wrong?"

Straightening a pile of papers on Carly's desk, Sara shrugged. "I guess I've got something on my mind. I'm sorry. I'll try to make sure it doesn't happen again."

Carly put a staying hand over Sara's. "We're friends. You know you can talk to me, don't you?"

Not about your brother. If Carly knew what had gone on between Sara and Daniel, she'd either string Daniel up by his toes or try to push Sara and Daniel into something impossible, such as marriage. Sara's stomach jumped. She managed a weak smile. "I know I can talk to you, and I really appreciate it, but this is just a little craziness that will go away in a week or so." She prayed it would.

Carly drummed her fingers on the desk. "Okay," she said reluctantly. "I need to ask a favor of you. I just got a call from Luke's school." Carly grimaced. "He has chicken pox and needs to be taken care of. But I have that important meeting with a representative from the National Tourism Association. If it were anyone else, I would cancel. Russ is in Chattanooga. I can't reach Daniel and the others, so I wondered if you'd handle Luke for a little while."

Sara hesitated, feeling immediately uneasy. Give her a mountain of paperwork and she could organize it in no time. Give her a business crisis and she'd manage it. She'd always, however, felt inadequate about dealing with children. "Carly, I don't know much about children. Especially sick children. What if he gets worse?"

"I'll give you the doctor's number. Luke is a great kid. Give him just about anything he wants to eat within reason, and he'll be happy as a clam. You have to take care of him only for the rest of the afternoon, then I'll pick him up around six and take him home."

"But what do you do with chicken pox? It itches, doesn't it?"

Carly shrugged. "You give him a bath. I need to pick him up from school." With violet eyes so like Daniel's, Carly looked at Sara beseechingly. "Will you do it?"

Thirty minutes later Luke was sitting in Sara's bathtub happily pretending her plastic cups and bowls were boats.

"Do you usually take a little nap in the afternoon?" Sara asked hopefully.

"Nap!" Luke screwed his face into a picture of horror and disgust. "That's for kindergarteners. I'm in first grade."

"Oh." Naps were obviously taboo, she concluded. "I didn't know if your fever was making you feel tired," she explained, trying to soften her offense.

"Nah." Luke poured water from the cup into the tub. "I'm just itchy. And maybe a little hungry."

A little hungry translated to two peanut-butter-and-jelly sandwiches, an apple, a banana, chips, and the last cupcake she had in the house.

He gave her a karate demonstration, which included a few bloodcurdling screams that left her ears ringing. Curious and funny, he was full of little-boy chatter about school, Garth and his mom, and a horse called Rapunzel. He allowed her to rub lotion on his itchy bumps. He made such a horrible face when she gave him the liquid antihistamine that Sara let him have an M&M to chase away the bitter taste.

They alternated checkers and reading with baths, and Sara lost her heart sometime around the third book when he asked if he could sit in her lap.

When five-thirty rolled around and Luke started getting a little cranky, Sara wondered if she should stall dinner or not. "Please don't scratch."

"But it itches," Luke wailed.

Her heart went out to him. The red marks now covered most of his trunk and neck. "I'm sorry. How about a bath?"

Luke groaned. "Another one?"

Sara thought for a minute. "I'll make a deal with you. You take a bath." She watched him frown and gently chucked his chin. "You eat dinner."

"And?"

"And we'll make chocolate-chip cookies afterward."

His eyes lit up. "Allll right! Let me at that tub."

Daniel knocked a little more loudly the second time on Sara's door. He'd gotten home an hour ago and listened to a half dozen increasingly frantic messages from Carly on the answering machine. The last one had asked him to pick Luke up from Sara's.

After Sara had firmly rejected him, Daniel had made a vow to get Sara Kingston out of sight and out of mind. Today, however, the luck of the draw wasn't running with him.

When no one answered the door, Daniel knocked once more, then tried the knob. It was unlocked, so he walked in. The smell of freshly baked cookies reminded him that he hadn't had dinner, and the sight that greeted him pulled at his heart.

Sara and Luke lay together on the sofa sleeping.

Wrapped protectively in Sara's arms, Luke gave a soft snore. A streak of flour dusted Sara's cheek. Her hair was tousled, her shirt wrinkled. And Daniel felt a dart of insane jealousy toward his new nephew. Daniel swore under his breath and took a couple of steps closer. There was something intimate about catching her asleep. Rumpled and defenseless, she wore no shields. It made him feel . . . strange. He cleared his throat. "Sara," he said in a whisper.

She still didn't budge, so he gently touched her shoulder. "Sara."

Her eyelids fluttered open, and he figured he'd better be ready to reassure her. While some women woke up soft and cuddly, others woke up looking and acting like shrews. A man couldn't be sure. Sara probably wouldn't be happy about him walking in without an invitation. If she felt startled, she might scream, and then Luke would wake up upset. It wouldn't help Daniel's nerves either.

He crouched down beside the couch, making sure she saw him immediately.

Her gaze met his, and she blinked a few times as if to focus. She smiled. "Hi, Daniel," she murmured in a sleepy, husky voice.

Soft and cuddly. Her smile was a knockout. He hadn't expected that. Confused, he frowned. "Hi."

She covered a yawn and eased one of her arms out from under Luke. "Did Carly send you?"

He nodded, watching the gentle way she handled Luke. She ran her hand over the little boy's forehead. "Still warm." A tiny frown knitted her eyebrows as she concentrated on getting up without waking Luke.

She wobbled a little as she straightened, and Daniel shot out a hand to steady her.

Her eyelids still droopy, she smiled again. "Sorry. I'm not too steady on my feet when I first wake up."

"It's okay." He kept his hand on her arm and noticed that she didn't try to move away. "Where do you want to go?"

"Kitchen. Coffee."

He led the way and nudged her into a chair. When she protested and tried to get up, he put his hand on her shoulder to keep her seated. He found the coffee, noticing it was a fancy blend, not the basic stuff he kept at home, and started the coffeemaker.

Watching her from the corner of his eye, he saw her sigh a few times and push her hair behind her ears. He wondered if she always woke up this way, full of soft sighs and vague smiles. She looked as though she needed to be held. He shoved his hands into his pockets to keep from doing just that.

The aromatic brew dripped into the glass pot, and Daniel located a mug. "Sugar or milk?"

Sara nodded.

He kept his grin to himself, adding milk and two teaspoons of sugar. He'd learned another little secret about Sara. She had a sweet tooth. He put the mug in front of her. "You're diluting the caffeine."

Sara shook her head. "The sugar's insurance. If the caffeine doesn't kick in, a sugar high will." Inhaling deeply, she lifted the steaming mug.

"Don't burn your mouth," Daniel cautioned.

She pursed her lips and blew, and Daniel thought he'd never seen anyone make drinking coffee look sexy. Someone ought to get her to do commercials.

She took a little sip, a few more, then looked at him. "Ninety seconds, and I'll start to make sense."

He took a seat opposite her and propped one foot on the opposite knee. "Don't rush on my account."

"Luke was very sleepy," she said after another sip.

"I don't think Luke was the only one."

At that point she seemed to come to her senses. She glanced down at her wrinkled shirt, quickly ran her fingers through her hair, and winced. "I'm a mess."

"Not too bad," Daniel said. "The flour on your cheek's a nice touch, and the mascara under your eyes is interesting."

Sara groaned and held up her hand. "Stop. You're worse than a mirror."

"The cookies smell great," he said, changing the subject.

Chagrin crossed her face. "I'm sorry. I should have offered you something." She stood, muttering to herself, "Ugly *and* rude." She glanced at the clock. "Have you had dinner?"

"No, but—"

She opened her freezer. "I don't suppose you eat Lean Cuisine. Wait a minute. Here's a Hungry Man's meal I picked up by mistake one time."

Daniel dragged her away from the freezer. "Sara, you haven't been rude. And if this is ugly, you're gonna have to work a helluva lot harder at it. You don't have to feed me dinner. I dropped by without an invitation to pick up Luke. If I don't get one of those cookies, though, I'm gonna get nasty."

Her lips twitched. "You really should eat dinner before cookies."

His gaze just this side of predatory, Daniel lowered his head closer to hers, knocking her pulse out of kilter. "I'll eat what I want. I'm a big boy."

If she weren't so fascinated, she would feel completely overwhelmed by him. Sara looked at his broad shoulders and superb body in feminine appreciation. "So you are." She heard the husky note in her voice and backed away. She cleared her throat. "Coffee, tea, or milk?"

Daniel's gut tightened at the expression on Sara's face. The woman had no idea what she brought out in him. "Coffee, tea, or me?" he invited in a deep voice, looking straight into her eyes.

Her stomach dipped. The air seemed to crackle between them. She had to block the urge to say, "You anytime." There was something just a little reckless in his eyes, something that called to her and seemed to say, honey-it-wouldn't-take-much. She exhaled slowly. "You don't look like a tea drinker. Coffee, milk, or ginger ale?"

"Sara," Luke called from the den.

"He's awake," she said, relief echoing in her voice. "Coming, sweetie," she called.

Wondering what it would be like if Sara called *him* sweetie, Daniel followed her out of the room.

Luke was sitting up, rubbing his eyes. "I'm all sweaty."

Sara put her hand on his forehead. "It's the fever." She unbuttoned Luke's shirt, and Daniel felt another ridiculous surge of envy.

"Do you want some ginger ale?" Sara asked. "It's time for your medicine again."

Luke made a face. "The gross stuff?"

"Yes. You want another bath?"

He shook his head adamantly, then his face lit up and he hopped off the sofa. "Uncle Daniel!"

"Hey, sport." Daniel crouched in front of Luke and gave him a hug. "I came to take you home."

"Do I get to sleep at your house?"

He shook his head. "No. I'm taking you to Carly's, and I'll stay with you till she gets there. Her afternoon appointment ran late."

After all her reservations about keeping Luke, Sara suddenly felt reluctant for him to leave. "He can stay here if you need him to. I've got his medicine and everything."

Daniel shrugged. "It's no problem. I thought we might watch a basketball game together." He nudged Luke. "Besides, he's family."

Luke beamed, and Sara's heart twisted.. "Of course. Well, let me get his things together." She bustled around, avoiding Daniel's thoughtful gaze. Within a few minutes they were all standing at her front door.

Daniel lowered his voice. "Are you okay?"

Startled that her mixed emotions were showing, Sara nodded emphatically. "Of course."

He frowned. "You seem kinda upset."

She gave him her best smile. "I'm not," she said, unsure of what her feelings were at the moment. She handed a small bag to Luke. "Here are your cookies. Since you helped make them, I thought you should have some. Just don't eat them all at once."

Luke peeked into the bag and grinned at her. "Thanks, Sara." He hugged her legs, and she reached down to return the spontaneous gesture, feeling her throat tighten up.

"Thank you. I hope you feel better soon."

She stood and handed another bag of cookies to Daniel. "Sorry it's not dinner."

"You could always give me a rain check."

Drawn to him much more than she wanted to be, Sara shook her head. "I'm *giving* you the cookies so you won't get nasty."

"Hey," he said, his eyes full of laughter, "I could get nasty if I don't get dinner. I'm a hungry man."

He was flirting. Straight-arrow Daniel Pendleton was trying to finagle a dinner from her with a flirty remark and a hot and heavy glance from those killer violet eyes of his. To her chagrin Sara found she wouldn't mind giving him dinner and a little more.

Mustering all her restraint, she opened the door and sweetly suggested, "If you're that hungry, then by all means stop by McDonald's on your way home."

"McDonald's doesn't have what I want, Sara," he said in a low, silky voice. "I'll wait for that rain check."

FIVE

Daniel stared at the roses in the florist's window. He'd spent the last two days with Sara sitting firmly in the back of his mind. She joined him for breakfast. She was there when he worked in the fields. She crossed her legs and watched while he talked with his brothers. And she was there in the damned red silk slip when he went to bed.

He'd spent an inordinate amount of time trying to figure her out. Unless his ego was talking, it was that old cliché "Your lips say no, no, but your body says yes, yes." She was susceptible to him. He knew it in his gut. She wanted him. It seemed that all she needed was a gentle shove and she would go right over the edge.

He grinned. And he would catch her.

Her nutty reasoning about why she couldn't get involved with him came to mind. Impatience sliced through him, and he felt his grin contort into a scowl.

The shopkeeper poked his head out the door. "Are you trying to make my roses wilt?"

Daniel felt self-conscious that he'd been caught. "No. I'm just looking. It's no crime to look, is it?"

The shopkeeper pushed back a strand of white hair on his balding head. He must have sensed a prospective customer. "It's no crime to look. It's no crime to buy either. The roses are on special today." After he imparted that information, he went back in his shop.

Daniel stewed in his juices for another two minutes, vacillating. After seeing the crack in Sara's resistance to him, he concluded that he needed to be a little more aggressive. Not a dozen roses, though. That would be overstating his case. One single red rose, he decided and pushed through the florist's door.

"It's for you."

Shaking her head, Sara looked at the single red rose in horror. She'd always hated roses since her affair with the senator. Her throat closed up.

Daniel extended it over her desk for her to take. The sweet aroma wrapped around her and squeezed her with memories and all the self-recriminations she'd tried to leave behind years ago.

Sara held up her hand. "No," she whispered, fighting a dozen overwhelming emotions.

"It's just a rose, Sara." Daniel's eyebrows furrowed together.

But it wasn't just a rose to her. It reminded her of the danger of wishing for things she wouldn't get. Not so much things, but people—such as a man who would love her, such as a family, such as children.

"I can't—" Her voice gave out when she looked at Daniel. If she were foolish enough to wish for a man to love her, she'd wish for Daniel. Appalled at the thought and deeply disturbed by the sight of the rose, Sara felt tears threaten. "Oh, no," she nearly wailed. Where had her control gone?

Totally confused, Daniel watched Sara stand. He caught sight of her watery eyes. "Are you allergic to them?"

Sara gave a little shake of her head. "No. I-I-" She bit her lip as if composing herself. "Thank you very much for the thought," she said in a wobbly voice. "But I don't like roses," she finished, her words fading into a broken whisper.

He watched her face crumple and felt his gut tie into a knot. He tried to reach for her, but she backed away, shaking her head.

She opened her mouth as if to explain, but the only sound that came out was a sob, then she stumbled out of the room.

That little feminine sob put a lump in his throat.

"What have you done?" Carly entered the room and glared at him. Apparently she had witnessed the last few seconds of the scene. Daniel hadn't noticed her. His complete attention had been focused on Sara.

Bemused, he shook his head and pointed at the rose. "I just brought her a rose. I swear. She started crying." He glanced at Carly. "Did you know she hates roses?"

"No. You must have said something."

"I didn't even ask her out for dinner."

Carly frowned. "I've never seen Sara close to tears."

"Yeah, well, she was crying just a minute ago. She looked upset." He felt helpless, and if there was one thing Daniel Pendleton hated, it was feeling helpless. "Maybe you'd better go check on her."

He stared at the offending rose. The sweet aroma teased his nostrils, but a bitter taste rose at the back of his throat. He swore under his breath in disgust. "Maybe it's not the rose she hates. Maybe it's me."

After that, Daniel stayed the hell away from Sara Kingston. It shouldn't have been all that difficult, between taking care of Erin's horse farm while she and Garth honeymooned, managing his own farm, and helping with the little emergencies that always seemed to come up during a major holiday like Christmas.

Just yesterday Daniel had received a call from Elbert Willis's very pregnant wife, Tina. Elbert had fallen off a ladder and broken a leg while he'd been stringing Christmas lights across the roof of his house.

Daniel fed and watered the livestock while Tina jiggled her one-year-old child on her hip. "This is really nice of you, Daniel. Elbert's daddy will be able to help us next week, but he's got a bad case of the flu right now."

"No problem. Troy, Jarod, or I can help you out till then. You okay for Christmas?"

Tina nodded. "I did my shopping through a catalog, and we're going to my Mom's for Christmas. She lives two counties over."

Daniel thought Tina looked awfully young to have two babies. She couldn't be more than nineteen. "You just make sure you stay near a hospital." He glanced over at a litter of six golden-haired puppies playing tag and nipping at each other. "They're close to being weaned. What are you gonna do with those?"

Tina smiled. "You want them?"

Daniel laughed. "No. I've got enough animals at my place."

"Well, spread the word," she said, following him

out the barn door. "The mom's sweet-natured, and there's nothing like having a dog to come home to. If you know anyone who wants an adorable puppy for Christmas, send them over here. I'll be happy to share."

During the drive home Daniel's mind drifted to Sara and what she was doing for the holidays. He wondered if she would be alone. It would be strange to be alone during such a time. Over the years he'd frequently resented his lack of privacy, but never during holidays. There was never a shortage of people at Pendleton family gatherings. Daniel wondered if Carly would invite Sara for Christmas dinner.

Sara probably wouldn't come. She seemed uncomfortable around his family, almost as if she wanted to join in, but wasn't sure how. The thought made his gut twist. She probably hated him for that rose. He still felt guilty about it.

A memory flashed through his mind of her sleeping on the sofa with Luke cuddled in her arms. Daniel frowned. There was more than one color to Sara Kingston's personality. She seemed satisfied with being single and childless, yet she had obviously loved taking care of Luke. A caring woman with no one to care for.

He wouldn't mind letting her care for him.

But she wasn't interested, he admitted with a dismissing snort.

———◆———◆———

Sara stared at the box, then at Troy. "What's this?"

His mouth lifted in a secretive grin. "Don't blame me. Check the note. It's from Daniel." He swallowed a chuckle and placed the box in her arms. "Merry Christmas." Then, before she could protest, he made tracks down her sidewalk to his truck.

Something shifted inside the box, and Sara looked at it suspiciously. She heard a little whine and felt trepidation. "He wouldn't," she muttered, stepping back inside the house.

Setting the box on the floor, she knelt beside it and tugged at the floppy bright red bow. Sara lifted off the top and stared into a pair of big brown eyes. The puppy let out a yip. Startled Sara jumped, muffling her own sound of surprise.

"Oh, Daniel, what have you done?" she murmured. She studied the wiggling little animal with the floppy ears, lolling tongue, and, to her dismay, huge paws. He cocked his head as if studying her in turn.

The gesture tugged at her heart. Sara sighed, and lifted him—she checked—it was a *him*. The bottom of the box was suspiciously wet. "What am I going to do with you? I always thought I'd be a cat person."

She brought him close, relishing the sensation of his soft fur. He gave her nose a quick lick, snuggled against her for a moment, then wiggled free to investigate his surroundings.

Sara glanced at the carpet, wondering how long it would be safe. Looking back at the box, she snatched the envelope and opened it.

Try this on for size. If, after two weeks, it doesn't fit, I'll take it back. He needs a tender touch. Thought you'd be the perfect choice.
—Daniel, who's still waiting for that rain check

She'd had Daniel Pendleton figured all wrong. She'd thought he was the most solid, sensible, upstanding man she'd ever met.

"He's nuts," she said to Troy later that night.

Troy laughed lightly. "I could have told you that."

Sara cradled the phone and looked at the latest puddle on her kitchen floor. "I really need to speak to Daniel, please."

"He's . . . ah, not available. I'll give him a message."

Sara frowned. "You've already said that three other times today. What am I supposed to do with this dog? You know, the Humane Society doesn't approve of surprising people with pets for gifts."

"Daniel knew you'd like this one."

"Daniel knew wrong. I have no idea what to do with this puppy."

"Get a gate for the kitchen. Put a soft blanket in the box—"

"The box is wet."

Troy snickered. "Get another box. If he won't go to sleep, try an alarm clock or a hot-water bottle, and call Daniel in two weeks."

"Troy—" Sara heard the click and knew she was talking to a disconnected line. Hanging up her phone, she admitted to herself that she needed to talk to Daniel for more than one reason. Sara cringed in embarrassment when she remembered how upset she'd gotten over the rose Daniel had tried to give her. He probably thought *she* was nuts.

He'd brought the rose at a weak moment for her, and it seemed she was having more than her share of those lately. Her feelings for Daniel were getting stronger. Denial wasn't working. Her mind needed no provocation to drift to thoughts of him.

Over the next few days Sara repeatedly tried to get in touch with Daniel. She simply could not keep the dog. She didn't have the space. She was gone during the day. And the animal yipped all night.

By the end of the week she'd bought a license tag, leash, an assortment of dog toys, and named him Pavi. She installed a gate in the kitchen doorway and sneaked home during lunch to take him for a walk. Whenever the cute little fellow greeted her, he wagged his tail so hard, he nearly lost his balance.

Sara faced the truth. She was now the owner of a dog.

Three days before Christmas, when everyone was finishing their last-minute shopping and doing their baking, the temperature shot up into the fifties, and Beulah County got twenty inches of rain within two hours.

Emergency volunteers were called in, and Carly and Sara closed the office to help at the community center. People brought in food and blankets. Medical personnel volunteered their services.

In the northern part of the county a few families had been trapped by the sudden deluge. Daniel and some other men worked late into the night to bring them to safety.

Sara was getting ready to leave the community center when Daniel finally showed up around midnight. Just seeing him kicked her nerve endings into overdrive. She watched him strip off the yellow rain poncho and push back the drenched hair from his head. Even from a distance she could see the weariness on his face. He must have felt her staring at him, because he looked up and held her gaze for several moments.

Her breath stopped. His face and body said he was tired, but the expression in his eyes said he wanted her. Badly. And Sara felt a tightening inside her. Her breasts felt heavy, her face went flushed, and her upper thighs tingled.

He gave a quick nod and looked away. Sara swallowed hard. She'd spent so much energy denying, avoiding, and rejecting her unwanted feelings for Daniel that she hadn't realized how much she'd missed him, just seeing him.

She felt uncomfortable about approaching him. What could she say that wouldn't sound idiotic? Especially since the last time she'd seen him, she'd burst into tears. Sara felt a flush of remorse and embarrassment creep up her cheeks. At a loss, she went to the food table where she'd been working with Carly most of the night.

"I see Daniel just walked in," Carly said.

Sara nodded as she filled a plate for the man in front of her. "Yes. I noticed."

"Bet he's hungry."

She stopped and looked at Carly. Her friend had just provided the solution to her dilemma. Sara felt a slow smile grow from the inside out. "I'm sure he is." She filled another plate, grabbed a canned drink, and made her way across the room.

Daniel sat talking to a couple of men about the flood. Sara thought about turning around and letting them finish, then shook off her cowardice. She took a deep breath and stepped forward. "Excuse me. I thought you might be hungry."

Daniel turned to look at her. Surprise flashed in his eyes. "Thanks. I am."

He continued to look at her but said nothing else. The two men silently watched. Sara couldn't think of a single intelligent thing to say. She felt ridiculous. Clearing her throat, she took a step back. "Well, I—"

Daniel quickly stood, his gaze nailing her feet to the floor. "Don't go."

Sara bit her lip, her gaze sliding to the onlookers.

Daniel narrowed his eyes. There was something different about her tonight. If he wasn't mistaken, he'd say she was a little more open to him, maybe a little softer, a little less guarded. *If* he wasn't mistaken. Sensing her self-consciousness, Daniel casually turned to the other men. "You guys are as hungry as I am. Go on and get your food, and we'll get together tomorrow morning."

The men muttered their agreement and ambled off.

"I hope I didn't interrupt something important."

"Nah. They just wanted to rehash a little." He pulled out a folding chair for her and waited for her to sit. He was also waiting for a stronger sign of what she wanted from him. Since that blasted rose incident, he felt as though he'd spent his last nickel at the fair and was thumbing his way home.

"Is everyone okay?"

He nodded and sat down. "We had a couple of close calls with some elderly people. They're in the hospital now but I think they'll be okay. The property damage is the problem." He shook his head. "You heard anything about Russ's place?"

Russ Bradford, Carly's husband, owned a catfish farm. "Carly says one pond flooded. But you know, he's got insurance so he should be okay. He made her stay here, and she's ticked at him right now."

Amusement lit Daniel's eyes. "If I know Russ, he'll find a way to get back in her good graces." He dug into the meal of fried chicken, mashed potatoes, and hot rolls.

"Long day?" she asked sympathetically.

He swallowed a bite and nodded. "Yeah. I probably look like hell."

His jeans and flannel shirt were wet and they clung to his muscular frame, emphasizing his broad chest, flat belly, and powerful thighs. Perhaps someone else would find that unappealing. That someone certainly wouldn't be female. Besides being affected by his impressive physique, Sara also admired his concern for other people. It weakened her already skimpy reservations about him.

"Sara, this is when you're supposed to lie and say, 'No, you don't look like hell. You look fine.' "

She looked at the ironic expression on his face, the dark shadow of his unshaven jaw, and the circles under his eyes. Leaning forward, she touched that rough jaw fleetingly. "No. You don't look like hell. You look like Beulah County's hero."

Daniel felt a rush of embarrassment. He cleared his throat, torn between rubbing his face against Sara's soft hand and pulling away. He liked having her admiration, but his feelings for Sara weren't particularly heroic. They were basic and selfish. He wanted her hot and naked beneath him.

She saved him from embarrassing himself further by asking him something else about the flood, then she carried the conversation while he ate. "I didn't realize this was such a busy time of the year for you. You've had a heavy workload lately, haven't you?"

Daniel shrugged. "It hasn't been that bad."

Sara's eyes widened. "Oh, really? That's not what Troy said."

"Troy has a bad habit of exaggerating. He—" Catching the skeptical expression on Sara's face,

Daniel stopped. Realization trickled in. She'd caught him. He cleared his throat.

"*Unavailable* is the word he used. Repeatedly." Sara smiled sweetly. "I should know. I've heard him use that word ten times during the last week. When you didn't return my calls, I wondered if you'd left the county."

Daniel grimaced. Not answering Sara's calls had been his greatest exercise in self-control. He'd wanted to badly. Just to hear her voice, even if she fussed at him about the dog, even if she said no. He set down his biscuit. "I knew that if you told me you didn't want the pup, I'd have to take him back and you wouldn't give him a chance to see how it would work out."

"Instead I suffered through seven nights of listening to him howl at the top of his lungs."

Daniel winced. "Could you put him outside?"

Sara looked at him as if he'd lost his mind. "So the neighbors could complain? It's been cold, Daniel. I don't know anything about puppies, but it can't be good for them to be outside in the cold."

"You want me to take him back?" he asked in resignation.

"No. Pavi and—"

"Pavi?"

"His name." Her lips twitched. "I named him

after Pavarotti, the opera star. We've come to a meeting of the minds." She thought of the puddles on her kitchen floor. "Sort of. I'm going to keep him."

Daniel was enormously pleased. "You like him."

Sara smiled. "How could I not?"

"I was right."

Sara nodded, and her expression became thoughtful. "About a lot of things."

Daniel felt the punch of her gaze clear to his gut.

"If you're not too busy . . ." she began and looked down. The way she twisted her hands was clear evidence of her edginess.

"I'm not." Daniel covered her hands with one of his own. The twisting stopped, and her gaze met his. Her eyes were full of emotion that changed like the weather, but the need he read was blatant. In his gut he felt the familiar, relentless rise of heat that no cold shower could ease. A wise man would sense the danger and would approach with caution. But he'd gone way past wisdom. There were layers of secrets enveloping Sara, and he wanted to peel them all off.

She turned her hand over and twined her fingers through his. "I was wondering if you'd like to take me up on that rain check for dinner." Her voice was soft and warm, as he imagined her body would be. "That is, if you're available."

"I'm available, honey," he growled without the slightest hesitation. He tightened his hand around hers. "Just name the time."

Sara tried to think. The sensible part of her knew she was headed straight for the frying pan by getting involved with Daniel Pendleton. The sensual part just didn't give a damn anymore. "The day after tomorrow is Christmas Eve," she managed. "The next day is Christmas." She lifted her shoulders. "I don't know."

Daniel had spent the last six months deciding what to do about Sara Kingston. He wasn't interested in waiting any longer. "Tomorrow night. I'll take you out."

Sara shook her head. "No," she said firmly. "You wanted a rain check for a meal. I'm fixing a meal for you."

Nearly groaning, he tossed back the rest of his soda. The only meal he wanted was her. The thought made his loins ache. Standing, he pulled her to her feet. "Come on."

Sara's gaze widened. "Where?"

"To my truck. To your car." He couldn't begin to explain the sheer necessity to feel her mouth beneath his. He nudged her toward the door. "Anywhere I can be alone with you."

"But—"

"Three minutes, Sara." He shoved the door open and led her outside. The cool mist hit his face, but didn't dampen his ardor. "All I'm asking for is three minutes. Where's your car?"

She pointed toward a Toyota three rows away. As they headed toward it, their shoes made crunching sounds in the gravel parking lot.

"It's not locked," she said breathlessly when they reached it.

Daniel opened the passenger door, slid in, and pulled her onto his lap. He slammed the car door shut. At her sound of surprise he took her face into his hands. "Three minutes."

SIX

It was a sexual kiss. No frills, little patience, full of need, and all-consuming. Sara's heart hammered in a staccato rhythm. She felt the press of his hard thighs beneath hers and his muscular chest beneath her hands. But for that moment the overriding focus of her existence was Daniel's mouth telling her without words that he wanted her more than anything in the world.

The intimacy of his tongue sliding past her lips and teeth to tangle with hers made her chest tighten. Tilting her head for better access, he was more aggressive than smooth. The blatant honesty in his every movement shook her to her core. She instinctively closed her lips around his tongue in a sucking motion. He gave a rough groan and nipped at her bottom lip.

He seemed to want to taste every corner of

her mouth, her soft inner lips, her teeth and tongue. His wanting made blood roar in her head and her nether regions pulse. She shifted and moaned, sliding her mouth first one way, then another against his. His arousal, pressed against her thigh, promised pleasure and fulfillment, making the achy, empty feeling between her legs almost unbearable.

Without hesitation she slipped her hand between their bodies and rubbed the hard ridge of flesh straining his jeans.

Daniel's hips moved convulsively, and suddenly she couldn't get close enough. She tugged at the button and zipper, all the while letting his open mouth consume hers. Her fingers found him, and he was like velvet-wrapped steel. When she closed her hand around him, he ripped his mouth from hers with a searing oath.

Sara's chest hurt with the effort to breathe. Through a haze of arousal she saw Daniel close his eyes as if he were in pain. "Don't. For Christ's sake, don't."

She couldn't stop, not with her body thrumming with his heady scent and the feel of him in her palm. Her thumb glanced the tip of his arousal.

Daniel jerked and swore again. Shuddering, he grabbed her hand and pulled it away.

His gesture jerked her back to reality. Her head abruptly cleared, and guilt surged through her. Her mouth had been so hungry, her hands had been sinfully curious, and her mind had abandoned her without a prayer. Appalled at her lack of control, she closed her eyes and tried to gather her wits.

"Sara," Daniel began.

Not wanting to hear whatever he had to say, she shook her head and swallowed. "No. Just give me a minute. I don't know—"

"Sara—"

Panic sliced through her. "Please!" Unable to face him, she bit her lip and stared at the steamed-up window. "Less than three minutes and I'm in your pants. I don't—"

Daniel gave her hand a quick jerk that stopped her desperate monologue and made her look at him. His eyes were black with passion. With exquisite deliberation he lifted her sinfully curious hand to his hot mouth and kissed it.

"You weren't doing anything I didn't want you to do." He kissed her hand again and gave a rough sigh. "But you know and I know that it wouldn't have taken much more and it would have been all over." His voice lowered. "I want to be inside you the first time."

Sara sucked in a deep breath. She cleared her throat. "I'm trying to get back some sort of control, and you're not making it easy for me."

"Honey, we passed control a long time ago." Twining his hands in her hair, he tugged her closer for a quick, possessive kiss. Shaking his head at his instantly renewed arousal, he set her into the driver's seat. "My three minutes are up." He gingerly eased up his zipper, fastened his jeans, and pushed open the car door. "I'll see you tomorrow night."

Sara's head was still spinning. "What time?"

He wrote six-thirty in the condensation on the windows and gave her one last heated glance. "Earlier if I can manage it."

Sara checked the beef tips one more time. Not overdone. Not underdone. Just right, she thought, stirring the meat while she set the burner on the lowest temperature. Rolls were warming in the oven. She'd uncorked the rosé wine to allow it to breathe. She'd hedged her bets by putting a couple of beers in the refrigerator just in case Daniel didn't like wine.

The table was set with her fine china and cloth napkins. She'd decided against candles because she didn't want the atmosphere too forced or staged.

She'd dressed in a carefully casual attire—a pink angora sweater and winter-white trousers. It was a good hair day. Everything should be perfect.

Everything would be perfect if the clock hadn't read seven o'clock. He'd told her six-thirty.

Tired of fidgeting, she went into the living room and sat down in a lounger. She pulled out a magazine and stared blankly at the pages. Her earlier sense of anticipation had fizzled during the last five minutes. Daniel was more reliable than this. There must be something wrong, she told herself. His tardiness wasn't a reflection on her. It was obviously due to external factors.

A niggling doubt, however, pulled at her. Her two serious romantic relationships had accustomed her to waiting for men. With the senator it had been a matter of waiting for him to call, waiting to see him, and waiting to be with him. With her husband it had been a matter of keeping his dinner warm while he worked late, keeping his bed warm when he was tired, and waiting in vain for his disapproval to wane.

In the back of her mind she'd always doubted that she'd been good enough for him. When he'd learned about the senator, his reaction had reinforced the belief. Still she'd waited and hoped that one day he would look at her without censure. Her hope had died with him.

She could hear the therapist's words: *You're a good person, Sara. You're lying if you tell yourself anything different. Make sure you don't let anyone else tell you differently either.*

Sara rose to her feet and tossed the magazine on the sofa. Damn right, she was a good person. And if Daniel Pendleton thought differently, he could forget any future rain checks, kisses in cars, or anything else.

Feeling a kick of energy after her little pep talk, she gave a huff of righteous pride and stomped around the den, repeating a few self-affirmations. She'd worked past her ebbing spirits when the oven timer dinged. Sara stopped, looking in the direction of the kitchen. The bread was ready.

And she had no guest to serve it to.

Three hours later while she wiped the counters, the phone rang. She considered not answering it. After spending most of the evening trying not to jump to unflattering conclusions about Daniel, she was in no mood to hear any half-baked excuses about why he wasn't here. Reluctantly she picked it up on the fifth ring. "Hello."

"Sara, this is Daniel," he said in a breathless rush.

His voice sounded so good that her heart squeezed in her chest. She exhaled in relief, and the unsettling, doubt-filled tension immediately left her body.

"It's been an awful night. Erin had an emergency with one of her mares, and I got tied up. I'm sorry, but I swear this is the first chance I had to call you."

She heard his earnest frustration, and suddenly

everything was okay. Sara recalled that several of Erin's horses were in foal. "Is the mare okay?"

"The mare is," he said quietly.

"And the foal?"

"She lost it."

Her heart sank. She could sense his disappointment. "I'm so sorry. Do they know what caused it?"

"Not yet. The vet's gonna run some tests. Damn, I hate to see this kind of thing happen during their first Christmas together."

"I know," she agreed. "At least they've got each other."

"Yeah."

"How's Luke?"

"Upset and confused."

She sighed, feeling helpless. "Is there anything I can do?"

"Nah. Carly brought over some food that everybody picked at. Everyone's just gonna hit the sack early tonight, especially Erin and Garth. I think they want to try to put it behind them as soon as possible."

"I'm really sorry."

"Yeah, and I'm really sorry that I didn't get to see you tonight."

Sara felt a twist in her stomach. "The mare was more important."

"Maybe." He took a deep breath. "But now I've

got to try to talk you into giving me a rain check on my rain check."

She felt the beginning of a grin. "Sounds complicated."

"Sounds *tough*."

Sara twirled the phone cord around her fingers. "Oh, I don't know. You'll probably think of something."

"It's damn lousy for a guy to push for a date and not show up. Most men wouldn't get another chance."

Sara stopped twisting the cord. "You're not most men."

A long silence followed, and on the other end of the line Daniel took a long time catching his breath. She affected him that way. He'd wondered if she would snub him. Hell, he'd been *nervous* about calling her because he feared he'd messed up his chances with her. Instead she knocked him for a loop with that last statement.

"I really wanted to see you tonight," he growled.

"Me too."

Her husky voice made his blood heat. "Tomorrow night."

"It's Christmas Eve. Your family—"

Daniel swore. He had to struggle to rein in his frustration. "Okay. December twenty-sixth at six o'clock."

"That's Sunday."

His patience long gone, he shook his head. "Tough."

On Christmas morning Sara slept in. She'd planned it that way. Sleeping late helped make long holidays feel shorter. She slipped on ancient slippers along with her silk robe, piled her hair on top of her head, and relished being a slob. After celebrating with a chocolate croissant for breakfast, she gave Pavi his food and an extra doggie treat. The puppy showed his gratitude by nearly licking her to death and puddling on the floor.

Sara cleaned up, then drew close the gate she'd installed in the kitchen doorway. She put a Christmas CD on the player, and opened the presents under her little tree. A sales rep who'd asked her out every time he passed through Beulah gave her a bottle of wine, and a travel agent in Chattanooga had sent her a huge box of fine chocolates.

She considered the wine. "Well, why not?" she muttered and went back to the kitchen to pop the cork. After pouring some into a crystal wineglass she took it with her to the den and alternated a few sweet chocolate candies with sips of the semidry wine. Sara sighed at the decadent flavor combination.

She'd saved Carly's gift for last—a gorgeous hand-embroidered sweater and an extra week of vacation in January. *Go someplace where you won't need this sweater*, the note said.

Sara smiled. Maybe she would. It was a gray day, and the weather made her think of past Christmases. She'd spent a few with her mother. Sometimes there'd been a man around, sometimes not. There'd been happier times spent with foster parents. Her thoughts wandered to the Christmas she'd spent alone because the senator had needed to be with his family. Mistresses, she'd learned, got romantic moments and presents, but they didn't get holidays.

She thought of Daniel and wondered if he would think of her the same way. Her heart gave a little wrench. He wanted sex with her. That was obvious. She wanted sex with him. She couldn't—and wouldn't—deny it. Was she getting herself into the same kind of relationship that had been her downfall before?

"Ridiculous," she said aloud, wanting to banish the distressing notion from her mind. Daniel wasn't a senator. He wasn't paying for her apartment, and she surely wasn't some naive, eighteen-year-old virgin. So what if they weren't broadcasting their relationship? They were both private people and wouldn't want others gossiping.

Something about it, though, left a bad taste in her mouth. Sara shook it off, gave Pavi the wrapping paper to shred, which he did with gusto all over the kitchen floor, while she removed from the freezer her turkey-and-dressing dinner. She refused to fix a meal with all the trimmings when she was feeding only herself.

The doorbell startled her, making her drop the frozen meal. Pavi started barking and trying to leap over the gate.

"Hush," Sara said. She looked down at the robe she still wore and grimaced at her appearance. The bell rang again, spurring her to the door.

To Daniel.

Speechless, Sara held her breath and simply stared at him. He wore a down jacket, red V-neck sweater, slim-fitting jeans, and boots. She jerked her gaze back to his face and caught the gleam in his violet eyes and a hint of a bad-boy grin curving his lips. Sara was acutely aware that he looked great, and she did not.

"Merry Christmas, Sara."

"Merry Christmas," she managed. "What are you doing here?"

He moved toward the door and nudged her to the side. "Picking you up for Christmas dinner with the Pendletons. Carly sent me. How's the hound?" he asked, nodding toward her barking dog.

"Fine. Carly must be confused," Sara returned, quite certain that neither Carly nor Daniel were confused. They were just pushy. "I told her I wouldn't be able to make it today." Remembering that her frozen dinner was in the middle of the floor, she headed toward the kitchen. "I've already got other plans."

Daniel matched her step for step. "What are you doing?"

Sara blocked the kitchen doorway with her body. "It's been a busy week, so I thought I'd have a quiet holiday. Tell Carly I said thanks, but—"

Daniel reached past her to pet Pavi and suddenly stopped. He spotted the frozen dinner and the bottle of wine at the same time. Unsettled, he looked at Sara again. She was in a silk robe. Her hair was sexily mussed, her chin had a smudge of chocolate on it, and she looked slightly alarmed, as if she'd been caught at something. Daniel had a sinking feeling in his gut. He wondered just what he'd interrupted. He wondered if someone was in her bedroom waiting for her. Jealousy slammed into him.

Past her shoulder in the den, he spied a wineglass and a box of chocolates. He cleared his throat and with enormous restraint said, "Did I come at a bad time?"

Sara looked in the same direction as his gaze and turned back to him with an overly bright smile and flushed cheeks. "Not really. I was just testing my Christmas presents."

He lifted an eyebrow. "Wine and chocolate?"

"I happen to like wine and chocolate," she said a little defensively as she stepped over the gate into the kitchen. "Not everyone in the Western Hemisphere gets up at the crack of dawn on Christmas morning and eats a huge breakfast and then eats a huge dinner."

"I didn't say they did."

She snatched the frozen turkey dinner off the floor, and before she could shove it into the freezer, Daniel took it from her hands and stared at her. If possible, she looked even more embarrassed than before. Bringing his libido and ego to heel, he tried to make sense of the situation.

He noticed there was only one turkey dinner, but he had to make sure. "I see one wineglass. Does that mean there was only one person drinking wine and eating chocolates when I rang your doorbell?" The image of feeding her chocolates raced through his mind and heated his blood.

Confusion clouded her wide eyes. "I—yes."

Daniel felt a rush of relief and put the turkey dinner into the freezer. "I'm always interested in other people's holiday customs. Just out of curiosity, what time did you get up this morning?"

Sara hesitated, frowning. "Ten-thirty, but—"

Daniel shook his head, remembering that he'd been up at six. "So this is Sara's version of Christmas. Sleeping in, then Perry Como, wine, and chocolates."

Sara stiffened. Her eyes flashed with anger. "I really don't appreciate—"

Daniel covered her mouth with his hand. He'd waited too long to touch her, so he plunged his other hand through the knot of silky hair on her head. "I just want to know if I can buy a ticket for next year."

Sara jerked her head back. "You haven't slept late a single day in your life."

"That's not true. I had the flu four years ago and didn't get up for three days."

Sara looked at the ceiling in mock disgust. "You wouldn't know what to do in bed past seven A.M."

Daniel gently pressed her back against the refrigerator. "Between the chocolates, wine, and you, I think I'd come up with something."

Sara bit her lip. "Get your hand out of my hair."

"You want me to put it somewhere else?" he murmured next to her ear. She wiggled against him, and Daniel nearly groaned. She always made him feel a raw edge of hunger. Why had he waited so long to appease his curiosity about this woman?

"Daniel—"

He gave in to one of his many cravings and kissed the chocolate smudge on her chin. "You know, Sara, I'm really hurt that you didn't invite me over for your holiday celebration."

"I thought," she said, swallowing and turning her head, "you'd be busy with your family."

Daniel ran his lips over her exposed neck. "So I missed breakfast. And it's already time for lunch. If I asked very nicely," he began, but got distracted by the taste of her skin.

Sara's hands hovered over his shoulders. Then, as if her resistance caved in, she dropped her hands to his chest. "Asked what?"

Daniel lowered his mouth to hers. The flavors of wine, chocolate, and Sara mingled and went straight to his head. He pulled away and was gratified to see her shortness of breath. "If I asked very nicely, would you join me for lunch?"

"I'm not dressed."

He lowered his mouth and suckled her lower lip. "I'll help you."

Her throaty laugh had the same effect as a stroke from her hand on his groin. She opened her mouth and gave him a kiss that made him feel as if he'd finally gotten every Christmas present he'd ever wanted. When his hands wandered to the deep V of her robe, she pulled back. Her eyes were hazy with desire. "Sorry you missed breakfast," she said in a husky voice.

"Does that mean yes to lunch?"

Sara's lips curved into a generous smile. "I guess you talked me into it." She eased away from him and turned toward the hall. "Give me ten minutes."

Daniel clasped her wrist. "I said I'd help."

"No." She wiggled her hand free. "Help yourself to the wine and chocolates while you wait."

Daniel took her suggestion, and when he sampled her gifts, he learned who the senders were. The notion that other men were vying for her attention didn't sit well, especially since he'd neglected to get her anything. Even Carly's note irritated him, making him wonder where Sara would go for her vacation and if she would invite someone to go with her.

Forty-five minutes later Sara and Daniel walked into the Pendleton home. All conversation between six brothers, a couple of spouses, a few dates, and several family friends ceased, and Sara was immediately bombarded by greetings.

"Sara!"

"Glad you could make it."

"We wondered when you'd get here."

Feeling a little overwhelmed, she gulped, said, "Merry Christmas!" then headed for refuge in the kitchen.

Carly was there checking the thermometer on the turkey in the oven. "Fifteen minutes," she called out to the group.

"Did you fix all this food?" Sara asked as she looked at the array of dishes set on the counter.

"Oh, no. Erin brought a few things, but I picked up double sizes of most of the casseroles from the grocery deli." Carly put down her oven mitts and hugged Sara. "I'm really glad you could come. I was afraid you wouldn't."

Her heart caught at the sincerity in Carly's voice. Sara truly was lucky to have such a friend. "I should have brought something."

Carly pulled away, her lips twitching. "You didn't have much time to fix anything, did you?"

"No. You didn't have to do this. Daniel said you'd sent him."

Carly arched an eyebrow. "Oh, really? I was on my way out the door when he suggested we flip a coin for the privilege of picking you up." She made a face. "He was in charge of flipping the coin, and I think he cheated. He didn't torture you or anything, did he?"

Sara felt blood rush to her face. Did Daniel's kisses constitute torture? "Daniel's not the kind to torture."

Carly shook her head and grinned. "You're being polite. I can tell by the tone of your voice."

"Who's being polite?" Daniel asked as he stepped into the room. He took a celery stick and stood beside Sara.

"Sara," Carly answered. "I asked her if you'd tortured her into coming today."

"Oh, yeah." Grinning, Daniel slid his hand into Sara's hair and gave one lock a little tug. "What did she say?"

Sara watched Carly open her mouth and decided to answer for herself. "I said you weren't the type to torture." She couldn't decide if she liked the glint in his eyes or not. She did know, however, that she liked his hands in her hair entirely too much. "*Torturer* isn't the right word."

"Then what's the right word?" Carly asked, clearly enjoying the exchange. "Make it a good one, like *arrogant*."

Sara nodded, still meeting the challenge in Daniel's gaze. "Maybe."

"*Gorgeous?*" Daniel offered.

Sara bit her lip to keep from laughing. "Perhaps."

"*Egotistical*," Carly suggested.

"Yes," Sara said without hesitation.

Irritation narrowed Daniel's eyes. He gave her hair another little secret tug. "*Irresistible.*"

"We'll see." Sara watched Daniel's eyes darken, and smiled. "You've both got great suggestions, but the word I was thinking describes both you and Carly.

Two pairs of violet eyes widened in amazement. "What?" Carly and Daniel demanded.

Sara laughed. *"Pushy."*

SEVEN

Just as Daniel and Carly recovered enough to respond, the timer went off. Literally saved by the bell, Sara thought.

Daniel gave her a glare that managed to combine threat with sensual promise. "We'll continue this later," he growled.

Sara made a tsking sound. "Pushy. Pushy."

He bent low to her ear. "Honey, what you've seen from me is patient, not pushy."

"Should I have used the term *overly assertive* instead?" she asked in a whisper. "Did you know that the first three letters in *assertive*—"

He put his thumb over her lips. "You've got a busy mouth."

Daniel could make Sara forget too easily all her resolutions about being conservative and not flirting or teasing. Staying out of trouble didn't seem to be an option when it came to him. "You don't like it?" she challenged.

He shook his head. "I didn't say that. I can just think of better uses for it."

So can I. Holding Daniel's gaze for a long while, she swallowed her rejoinder. Someone cleared his throat, and Sara jerked her head around to find Troy staring in amusement. At that moment she would have traded a box of Godiva chocolates for a paper bag to put over her head.

Carly, God bless her, announced the turkey was ready, and she was nearly stampeded by her brothers. Everyone filled their plates, then took a seat at the huge dinner table. Daniel, at the head of the table, offered the blessing.

Sara, ensconced between Jarod and Troy, felt the return of underlying uneasiness about being among the Pendletons during this special holiday. They all seemed so comfortable with each other. They all seemed to belong. Sara knew she didn't.

She was an intruder, she realized, as she listened to the different conversations and watched the family. Somebody asked Luke about one of his pet chickens while Carly cut the little boy's meat into small bites. Daniel offered Russ the butter and started a discussion about the effects of the flood, and Brick, Ethan, and Nathan were discussing a camping trip they'd taken last summer. Erin seemed a little withdrawn until Garth wrapped a supportive arm around her and whispered something in her ear. Her mouth lifted in a grin.

Sara looked away and tried to concentrate on her food.

"How's the pup?" Troy asked.

Sara started, then smiled. "Wet, loud, and adorable."

"Strange combination," he said, shaking his head.

At the friendly overture, Sara relaxed a bit. Jarod asked about how she liked Beulah County, and they soon got into a discussion on the different hangouts in Chattanooga, since Jarod had lived there during his college years.

"You don't have a southern accent," Jarod observed. "Is your family from Chattanooga?"

Sara felt a sliver of discomfort. "My former husband was."

"Oh, that's right," Jarod said. "Where do your parents live?"

Everyone seemed to take a breather from talking at that particular moment, and with the exception of the sound of silverware meeting china, the room was silent.

Sara cleared her throat and glanced around to find several people looking at her expectantly. She felt horribly awkward. "They, uh, used to live in Minnesota. They're dead now," she added more quietly.

Jarod faltered. "Well, I stepped right into that one. I'm sorry. Sounds like you have something in common with us," he said, referring to the fact that both Pendleton parents were dead.

Sara darted a quick look at Daniel. His inscrutable expression did nothing to alleviate her anxiety. "A little bit in common," she said lamely, in an effort to help Jarod feel better. That they were all human beings was about all she had in common with the Pendletons, she supposed. Jarod's remark only served to emphasize that fact, and Sara abruptly identified where her underlying uneasiness originated. She'd thought she was uncomfortable around the Pendletons because she wasn't a member of their family, but that was only part of it.

The truth of the matter was that among these connected, loving people, Sara Jean Kingston felt like a complete fraud.

One more try, Sara thought, as she stirred the simmering beef tips. She wore the same pink sweater, same winter-white slacks as last time. At five fifty-five the doorbell rang. Pavi barked from behind the laundry-room door. Sara ignored him. She refused to dodge his puddles during this meal!

She opened the front door, and Daniel's tension rolled over her like a wave. He wore a suit and a wary, careful expression on his face. He tentatively offered the bunch of violets in his hand. "These okay?"

Her heart turned a flip. Despite a jab of embarrassment over her reaction when he'd given her a rose, Sara smiled and accepted the gift. He was uncomfortable, and if there was one thing she'd learned, it was how to put a man at ease. For once she knew what to do with Daniel Pendleton. "Violets are wonderful." She took his hand and pulled him into the room. "And you look great."

"I'm overdressed," he grumbled, wishing he'd worn something more casual.

"I like your tie."

"You can have it." He tugged it loose and followed her into the kitchen, appreciating the sight of her great rear end. He wondered how long he could watch and refrain from touching.

Sara laughed. "Relax. Take off your jacket and shoes. This is just a rain-check dinner with Sara Kingston."

Daniel was anything but relaxed. He was wound up so tight from arousal, anticipation, and tension, he felt crazed. He shook his head. "This is the beginning of my forbidden affair with a wild woman."

Sara stopped in the midst of putting the flowers in a vase. Had he offended her? Then she smiled, an almost taunting smile.

"We'll see," she said noncommittally. "Beer or wine?"

"Beer," he replied. Her comment ate at him. "What do you mean, 'we'll see'?"

Sara popped the top on the beer and handed it to him. "Just what I said. We'll see. We've got lots to do. You've got to drink this beer. Then we've got to eat dinner, and you'll have to tell me how wonderful it was. Then we eat dessert and—"

"*Lady, give me a break.*" Daniel meant it. He knew he was coming across as smooth as a rough ride on a bronco, but he had to know how to gear himself. Every fiber of his male being said skip the food and take the woman.

Sara gave a sigh. She stepped closer, and Daniel felt his pulse throb in every erogenous zone in his body. She shook her head and pulled off his tie. "You really need to relax. Sit down and let me tell you what I bought today."

"Sara—"

"Just listen." She pulled out a chair and gave him a nudge. When he didn't move, she glared at him. Daniel sat down, resigned to be driven straight up the wall.

She pushed off his jacket. "I went to the new department store today. They have a great cosmetics section."

She began to rub his shoulders, and the sensation of her fingers on his tight muscles made the inane conversation more bearable. "Good?" she asked.

He gave an appreciative groan.

Sara laughed, and the husky sound was another reminder of another discomfort he wished she'd take care of.

"I don't suppose you frequent the cosmetics department," she continued.

"Not lately," he said dryly.

"Cosmetics companies know how to go for the jugular. Women can be tempted by claims of how much all these products can do for them. For example, my new lipstick . . ."

She sifted her fingers through the hair on his nape until Daniel was sure every nerve ending in his body was standing at attention. Surprisingly enough, her new lipstick teased his imagination. "What about it?"

"It's called . . ."

He heard the hesitation in her voice and turned. "What?"

She unfastened the top button of his shirt, her hazel eyes focused on his neck. " 'Sensual.' The company promises that it will stay on my lips until I take it off. I can't drink it off. I can't eat it off. And you," she said finally lifting her sultry, challenging gaze to his, "can't kiss it off."

She put her thumb on his bottom lip, and Daniel felt his mouth go desert dry. Her scent wrapped around his senses. He noticed how the V-neck of the sweater she wore revealed just a hint of cleavage. Nestled on a long chain between her breasts, where he'd like to put his mouth, was a cluster of pearls. *Punch. Punch. Punch.* One more and he'd be down for the count. He cleared his throat.

Sara dampened her lips with her tongue.

Boom. That was it. He tumbled her into his lap. "I could dedicate myself to a whole night of disproving that kind of claim."

"Is that so?"

He kissed the corner of her mouth, just to tease her as she'd been teasing him. Her swift intake of breath was gratifying. "You know how it is with the oldest son. A hardworking overachiever type like me won't stop till the job is done."

He wrapped his hands around her waist, lowered his head, and covered her mouth with his. He settled his lips first one way then another, the better to smudge her lipstick. Or was it because he wanted intimate knowledge of every centimeter of her lips?

At her soft sigh he forgot the game and dipped his tongue past her teeth, savoring her flavor. He felt a rush of satisfaction when her hands crawled up and clung to his shoulders and her breasts rubbed enticingly against his chest. Her tongue coupled with his, thrusting, dancing, and Daniel thought he could spend the next hour just kissing her.

He probably would have if she hadn't pulled back. Swaying, Sara visibly caught her breath and ran her not-so-steady index finger around his mouth. "Not yet," she said, looking a little stunned.

Daniel swallowed. "Not yet what?"

"You haven't kissed off my lipstick."

Daniel looked at her still-tinted lips. "Well, hell, give me another minute or two—"

Sara shook her head and stood on shaky legs. "Drink your beer while I serve dinner."

Daniel thought pouring the beer over his head would be more effective. "Dinner?" He caught her hand.

She nodded slowly, her eyes still hazy. "Remember," she said, gently prying his fingers off hers. "Getting there's half the fun."

The meal passed in an ebb and flow of excruciating anticipation. Just when he relaxed, Sara would do something like lick her lips or fiddle with the necklace that lay between her breasts, and Daniel would start feeling crazy all over again.

"Dessert okay?" Sara asked.

Daniel didn't have to put much effort into appreciating the chocolate mousse topped with whipped cream and raspberries. "Delicious. Where'd you learn how to make it?"

Sara's gaze went shuttered. She set her spoon into her bowl. "I, uh, took cooking lessons a long time ago. Someone gave me the lessons as a present with the agreement that I prepare a meal for him when I completed the course." She picked up her wine and took a deep drink. "I forgot most of the recipes, but I guess the chocolate mousse stuck." She gave a wry, forced smile. "The way it sticks to the hips."

The joke was weak, and Daniel found himself wondering about the shadows that came and went in Sara's eyes at odd moments. She'd let him know that she wasn't pure. The knowledge didn't put him off. Instead it excited him, made him feel free. But tonight, he thought, rubbing a finger over his lip, he didn't like the man who'd paid for the cooking lessons because Daniel suspected there'd been more than one meal involved. That relationship had obviously made her sad. And Daniel didn't want to make Sara sad. He wanted to make her smile. He wanted to hear her laugh. He wanted a lot.

Leaning across the table, he scooped some dessert onto her spoon and lifted it to her mouth. "I like the way it sticks to your hips."

Sara fluttered her eyelids in disbelief. "Right." But she opened her mouth and let him feed her.

"I do," he insisted. "And I ought to know, since I've spent a lot of time watching your—"

Sara swallowed, shaking her head. "Daniel—"

He pushed another spoonful past her lips. "Did you know that your rear end is perfectly heart shaped? Of course I've had to conduct this study from a distance, but if I set my mind to it, I could come up with your hip measurement."

Sara lifted her hand in alarm. "Please don't. You've already guessed my weight. That's enough."

"For who?" He clasped her wrist and tugged, bringing her out of her chair and into his lap.

"For both of us?" Her heart hammering against her ribs, Sara watched unequivocal determination flare in Daniel's eyes.

"I drank my beer. I ate the meal, and it was wonderful. Dessert was delicious. Getting here's been half-fun and half-torture. I need to get back to work on smudging your lipstick. I need to figure out your hip measurement." His lips lifted in a lazy, sexy smile that made her breath catch. "I don't plan on leaving here until I figure out exactly how your body fits together."

He clasped her waist, then boldly worked his big hands down to her hips and lower still to her thighs. The tension inside her grew tighter and tighter, spreading to vulnerable feminine places he hadn't touched.

"And how it's gonna fit with mine."

Sara leaned her head against his solid chest and moaned. "Oh, Daniel. I knew you'd be a horrible tease," she whispered.

"I'm not teasing, honey. I'm promising." He shifted her in his arms, stood, and carried her down the hall. "Which way?"

No man had ever carried her, she thought, swallowing over a lump in her throat. The chivalrous gesture nearly rendered her speechless. "Right."

He kissed her at the same time that he let her body slide down the front of his until her toes touched the floor. His tongue eased into her mouth, and her bones began to melt. One of his hands slipped under her sweater to the small of her back, while the other went to her bottom and pulled her to him. He rocked against her in a heady rhythm that sent sensation pooling into her nether regions.

When she echoed his movements, he groaned against her lips. "You taste like chocolate and raspberries and . . ."

His hand slid to her breast, and Sara sucked in a deep breath. "And what?" she asked breathlessly, craving the way his voice made her nerve endings jump and shimmy. Her body undulated against his, cradling his arousal between her thighs.

Daniel shuddered. "Oh, Sara, you taste like every secret erotic dream I've ever had," he whispered, and his confession sent an unbearable thrill throughout her.

He tugged her sweater over her head and tossed it on the bed, then looked at her. Sara knew what he saw. Her pink lace bra couldn't conceal the budding of her nipples. For a second she felt self-conscious. It had been a long time for her, and somehow, with

Daniel, she felt very different. She put her hand over the necklace and started to remove it.

His hand stayed hers. "Leave it on," he murmured, still staring at her breasts until she felt the tips harden even more.

He took a deep breath and lifted his gaze to hers. "How do I get you out of these pants?"

She smiled, moving slightly away from him. "All you had to do was ask."

He watched her unbutton, unzip, and smoothly step out of the slacks while the pearl necklace swayed against her breasts. The little scrap of pink lace hugging her hips drew his gaze like a homing device. He could rip it apart in seconds, and the thought of touching her where she was moist and hot nearly sent him over the edge. He clenched his hands to keep from grabbing her and taking her right then. How could she be so smooth when he felt worn and ragged from restraint? He opened his mouth to tell her how beautiful she was, but nothing came out.

Sara laid her hands on his chest and looked at him with the age-old mystery of Eve in her eyes. "This is a little inequitable, don't you think?" She undid his buttons one by one. The sensation of her hands on his chest made his heart pound.

She pulled out his shirttails, moved her hand to his belt, and hesitated. "I guess it's my turn to ask. How do I get you out of these pants?"

"Give me half a minute," he growled, dispensing with the belt, then shucking both his pants and briefs in one swift motion. He felt her gaze travel from his shoulders, down his chest, to his aroused manhood. She looked at his legs and feet, and Daniel held his breath, hoping like hell she liked what she saw.

Her expression said she wasn't intimidated by his size. She was excited by it. She stepped forward and rubbed her cheek against his chest. "You're a beautiful man, Daniel."

The comment surprised him. He plowed his fingers through her hair. "Me? You're the one who's beautiful. Hair like silk, skin like satin, and your nipples, they remind me of those raspberries."

Sara looked down, undid her bra, and shrugged it off. Daniel lifted the necklace over her head. The chain still retained her body heat. He closed his palm around it, then hung it over the knob of her bed headboard.

He'd barely turned back to her before she rubbed those raspberry nipples against his rib cage. The sight and sensation was too erotic for words.

Something inside Daniel broke free, and his hands went wild. Cupping her breasts, he thumbed her nipples while he lowered his head to kiss her. She welcomed his tongue into her mouth, responding with the same intensity he felt. Her hands gripped his shoulders as she arched against him. He slid his hands inside her panties, over her bottom, then between her legs where she was warm and wet. He slipped a finger inside her.

Sara gasped.

"Too fast?" God, he hoped not.

"I don't think"—she shook her head, clenching her thighs to keep his hand there—"there's any help for it."

He was trying not to lose it completely. He was trying to concentrate on making sure she was ready, but her heady scent had his senses swimming. The look in her eyes was the kind a man would beg for, and he was throbbing with the need to replace his finger with the part of him that was aroused to the point of pain.

She wrapped her hand around him, and his knees nearly buckled.

He sucked in a quick, sharp breath. "S-S-S-Sara."

She rubbed her thumb over the tip.

Daniel swore.

She removed her hand, and he swore again.

"I've got something in the drawer by the bed," she murmured, backing away from him, her eyes dark with passion.

Hating the space between them, he dragged her back and wondered what she was talking about. Then it dawned on him. Protection. He'd brought a couple of condoms in his pocket.

She pulled him with her, found the plastic packet, and tore it open. Then she gave him a shove so that he sat on the bed, and she bent over and smoothed the thin sheath over him. He realized she'd done this before, but he banished the thought immediately. She was his tonight. That was all that mattered.

Her breasts bobbed inches near his face, tempting him, and he took one tip into his mouth.

Sara moaned in pleasure and stroked him in rhythm with the sucking motion of his mouth. His hands were restless, making her burn with a heat that would rival the fires of hell. She wanted him badly. That want was quickly escalating to a need that pulsed between her thighs and made her heart ache in a strange, confusing way.

He suckled her nipple again, tightening the need and making her feel a little desperate. "Daniel." Sara heard the sound of distress in her voice and swallowed hard. "I—"

Suddenly he lifted his head, leaned back, and pulled her so that she fell on his chest. Before she could catch her breath, he rolled her beneath him. He shifted between her legs, and she felt his arousal, thick and hard, poised at her entrance.

She'd never been more aware of her vulnerability, but she sensed he was holding back for her. The teasing and not quite having nearly made her beg.

His hungry gaze fell over her, and he briefly shut his eyes as if he, too, were struggling for control. "I'm about at the end of my rope, Sara," he said, lifting a trembling hand for her to see.

"That makes two of us," she said breathlessly, and placed her own trembling but smaller palm against his.

He looked at their matched palms and, one by one, twined his callused fingers with her smooth ones. Then he looked up and stared deep into her eyes. His expression shook her. Something powerful passed between them, something she could barely fathom.

Then slowly, deliberately he pushed himself inside her, stretching and filling her.

"God, you're tight," he whispered, savoring the moment.

It was true. He was big, and it had been a while for her, so Sara had the odd feeling of having too much, but still wanting more. He pulled back, and she arched against him, wanting him to stay inside her.

"What is it?" he asked, pushing a strand of hair from her face.

His gentleness made it worse. Sara felt beads of perspiration gather on her forehead. "You feel good inside me. Don't—" She broke off when he pushed in to the hilt.

He lowered his mouth to her ear. "Don't what?"

Everything about him felt so wonderful, his voice, the beating of his heart against hers, his legs against her inner thighs. She felt herself straining toward him. "Don't stop," she said, the words more of a whimper than a command. Need made her bold, though. She urged his hips down with her hands and arched into him.

His face was a study of pleasure and pain. "I couldn't stop if I tried."

He covered her mouth with his, and his tongue echoed the pumping of his pelvis. The slide of his flesh in hers made them both slick with perspiration. He whispered words of encouragement that made her rise against his thrusts in a faster rhythm.

The tension inside her grew so tight that she hurt. Closing her eyes, Sara turned her head to the side.

"No." His husky voice drew her back. "I want to see your face." He slipped his hand between them. "I want you to look at me."

Holding her with his gaze, he caressed the tiny button of her femininity until she bucked against him and began to shudder uncontrollably.

His face lit with rapture, he gave a rough groan and thrust heavily, catching the wave of her ecstasy and riding his own. When she was still trembling moments later, he held her tight as if he were trying to prevent her from falling apart. Sara bit her lip against an appalling urge to cry. It had been too wonderful. Another layer of restraint fell from between them, and for the first time in her life she felt utterly possessed.

EIGHT

"*Lord.*" Daniel felt as if he'd just discovered sex for the first time. Struggling for breath, he looked at the woman in his arms with awe. She was so incredibly responsive, he thought. She was still clinging to him.

She was also still shaking. Daniel's gut twisted. He turned to his side, pulling her with him. "Hey. Hey. Are you okay?"

Sara burrowed her face into his throat but didn't say anything.

He stroked her hair in a soothing motion. "Sara?"

"Give me a minute."

Daniel tensed. She sounded all choked up, making him fearful that she was crying. He counted to sixty and lifted her chin. Her dazed but tear-free eyes met his.

He felt a punch of relief and something else. She looked the way he felt. He swallowed hard and tried to grin. "You didn't tell me I was going to need a pacemaker."

Her expression solemn, she shook her head. "I don't know what to say."

"You can say you're okay."

"I'm okay," she said in a quiet, uncertain voice. She took a deep breath, then her gaze skittered away and she bit her lip. "I just remembered I need to let Pavi out. I meant to after dinner, but . . ."

"I distracted you," Daniel finished for her. "I'll do it. It won't take—"

"No!" Sara worked free of his arms and sat up. "You're the guest. Do you want something to drink? Wine? Beer? Coffee?" She started to stand, but Daniel caught her around the waist and pulled her down.

"Sit tight. You've done enough tonight." He rose and stretched. "I think I can manage coffee."

Heedless of his nudity, he walked from the room.

Sara was in a quandary. She'd mentioned Pavi as an excuse to get away from the scent of their lovemaking, to get out of bed, where her defenses had been stripped. Going to bed with Daniel had been more than a mutually pleasurable experience. His kindness had seemed more personal, as if he actually cared for *her*.

Sara made a face. Daniel cared for everybody, she reminded herself. Something, though, about the way he looked at her made her wonder if he saw her as something more than the wild woman. The notion frightened her, and if she were honest, she'd admit it thrilled her too.

Did she want him falling for her? Did she want to ruin another good man? her conscience chided. Did she want to try again?

She saw him step through the doorway carrying a mug and a package of cookies. He wore a grin that charmed her worries away. She couldn't contain an answering smile. "I wish I had a camera. This would make an interesting picture. Nude man with coffee and Oreos. What would your brothers say?"

"They'd say, 'You lucky dog,' because if they said anything else, I'd have to beat 'em up. Here." He set the mug on the night table. "With sugar and cream," he said before she could ask. "Want a cookie?"

"Sure. Where's your coffee?"

"We're sharing," he answered with a sly look.

"Oh." Wondering what he was planning, Sara took a quick gulp.

"Speaking of my brothers, it crossed my mind that dinner at Sara's house is different from dinner at Daniel's house. What did you think of Christmas?"

Sara's gaze fell to the bedspread. "It was fun, noisy, and friendly. Your family seems close. It was very nice of you and Carly to invite me."

Daniel heard the beginnings of that polite, distancing tone in her voice, but he forged ahead anyway. "Did Jarod's questions bother you?"

She shifted and tugged the bedspread over her. "They were normal questions."

He put his thumb under her chin and lifted it. "We've just been as close as two people can get. Can't you talk to me?"

Her eyes looked defensive. "Just because our bodies have been close doesn't mean I'm going to bare my soul too."

Daniel felt as if he'd been slapped. He pulled his hand away. "Sorry."

Sara sighed and shook her head. "No. I'm sorry. I shouldn't have snapped at you. I guess I'm feeling a little strange." She gestured vaguely with her hand. "This being our first time and everything."

Daniel narrowed his eyes, feeling a twinge of uneasiness in his gut. "Was it what you expected?"

"No."

His heart seemed to stop beating.

She sighed. "It was more. . . . Oh, I don't know how to describe it. You were more than I expected."

His heart settled back into its normal rhythm. "Do you mean my body was more, or something else?"

Sara nodded. "Yes, your body." She blinked. "Yes, something else.

"Sara—"

She put a finger to his lips. "I told you earlier I didn't know what to say. I still don't. But you're more than I expected." Her gaze fell over him in a warm, womanly way that made him feel incredibly glad he was a man. "You've got a great body and I haven't really had the kind of opportunity I'd like to explore it." She lifted the package of Oreos out of his hand and placed it on the nightstand with her coffee. Then, slanting a sultry look at him, she put her hand on his chest and swirled her fingers through the spray of hair. "Do you mind if I explore now?"

Every nerve ending in his body went on alert. Daniel sucked in a deep breath and flattened his hand over hers. "If I didn't know better, I might think you don't want to answer my questions. I might think you're trying to distract me."

Sara silently laid her head on his chest. Her hair felt silky against his skin and her breasts teased his belly, bringing him another twist of pleasure.

"Nothing to say?"

"I take the fifth. You don't want me to . . . explore?"

The woman should be put behind bars for her seductive abilities. She didn't seem the least bit concerned about her nudity. If he could just get her to trust him enough to share a few more of her secrets. . . . One thing at a time, he decided, feeling his loins thicken with desire.

He squeezed her hand. "I'm more than willing for you to explore, but you need to remember about the Pushy Pendletons. I'll be asking those questions again, and next time I'll be expecting answers." He tossed the bedspread off the lower half of her body and lay down next to her. He went one step farther in making himself appear defenseless by releasing her hand and spreading both of his on either side of his body. "Do your worst."

"Just remember," she said, lazily stroking her tongue across one of his nipples, "you asked for it."

Three hours later Daniel walked out to his truck. He would have liked to stay the whole night, but Sara didn't want the neighbors talking. His legs felt like stretched-out rubber bands. His cardiovascular system felt as if he'd run a marathon. His brain had turned to mush, and he was ridiculously delighted with the fact that there wasn't a smidgen of lipstick left on Sara Kingston's delectable mouth.

It took him three tries to get the truck in gear, and he still had to fight the overwhelming temptation not to go back to the house for more.

Whatever he'd expected from Sara Kingston—

and he'd expected a lot—he hadn't expected to feel such intensity of sensations. She'd tickled, teased, taunted, tormented, and satisfied him in a way he'd never before experienced.

He drove through the dark night, concentrating on the hours he'd spent with her. He was beginning to comprehend the possibility of how she could ruin a man, although Daniel didn't put himself in the ruinable category. He was too self-disciplined and sensible to let a woman destroy him, but the fact remained that Sara Kingston packed a punch. She had been so utterly focused on pleasing *him*. She'd made him feel like the most important man in the world.

The only thing that grated on him was the way she'd avoided answering his questions. Maybe it should have been enough that he had possessed her body and she had possessed his. After all, that had been his goal, to have her sexually. But something about her made him crave more.

Pulling into his driveway, he made a promise to uncover all her secrets. Then, he sensed, he would feel satisfied. Then he wouldn't have this edgy I-think-about-her-too-much feeling. Then his hunger for her would wane.

He got out of the car and walked to the front door, careful to keep the screen door from slamming as he entered. Not wanting to wake his brothers, he made his way quietly to the large den, where he found Troy asleep on the sofa. He turned off the TV.

Troy sat up. "That you, Daniel?"

"Yeah. Why don't you go to bed?"

Troy yawned, stood, and stretched, then squinted his eyes at Daniel. "Your hair's all messed up."

"Thanks," Daniel said dryly.

"Where are your socks and tie?"

"In my pockets." Daniel tried not to grind his teeth. Troy could be such a pain, he thought, and decided to head for the privacy of his own room.

Troy laughed, following him down the hall. "Looks like you had some night."

Daniel ignored his brother and opened the door to his bedroom.

"So you gonna tell me about it? Was Sara a great lay, or what?"

A rush of fury sped through his veins. He whirled, grabbing Troy and forcing his brother against the wall. "I don't ever want to hear you say that word in the same sentence with Sara's name again. What goes on between her and me is private. Do you read me? It's none of your damned business. And you'd better keep your stupid mouth shut around her unless you have something polite to say." Daniel saw his brother's expression of horror and dropped his hands.

Disgusted with Troy and with his own violent reaction, Daniel turned away.

"Sorry," Troy murmured.

"Okay," he said. "Get some sleep." Daniel walked into his room, shutting the door behind him. He gave a heavy sigh and looked at the floor. His emotions were more out of control than he'd realized. If this was what happened after one night with Sara, he was going to have to be very careful in the future, because it sure as hell wasn't going to be his last night with her.

She'd seen him every night except two since the first time they'd made love. They'd start out just talking or sharing a meal, but they couldn't seem to keep their hands off each other and always wound up in bed.

Tonight, however, due to her monthly cycle, she wasn't in the mood to make love. So she left a carefully worded message with Troy that she was tired and would see Daniel in a day or so.

She'd had a long day at the office followed by a volunteer committee meeting to discuss starting a food closet for Beulah County. There was a relentless, depressing rain falling outside, and if she were sensible, she'd stay away from chocolate and salt, take a nice hot bath, and go straight to bed.

But on the way home she picked up a bag of

cheese popcorn, three chocolate-filled doughnuts, and a videocassette of *Dr. Zhivago*.

After taking a hot bath she put on her oldest flannel nightgown and planted herself on the sofa with the popcorn, a doughnut, and the remote control. A third of the way through the movie she started bawling.

About the time she reached for the tissues, the doorbell rang. She quickly blew her nose and ran to the door. Peeking through the window, she swore.

Sara cracked the door open. She didn't want to invite him in. "Hi, Daniel. Did you get my message?"

"Yeah." His voice was dark and confrontational. "Troy said you were tired of me."

Sara fought a surge of frustration. "I didn't say I was tired of you. I just said I was tired."

"Are you gonna let me in?"

Daniel's hair and suede jacket were wet, and he looked as if he had every intention of camping on her doorstep if she didn't invite him in. She sighed and swung open the door.

Emanating displeasure, he stepped in and stood in the hallway for several moments, not saying a word. Sara's sniff broke the silence, and he studied her face. "Have you got a cold?"

She sniffed again, imagining the sight he beheld. Her eyes would be bloodshot, her nose red, and her skin splotchy. "No. I always cry when I watch *Dr. Zhivago*."

"You've been crying!" He was obviously horrified.

"Yes. Daniel, this isn't a good night for me. I'm worn out and I don't really feel like"—she waved her hand, searching for the right word—"entertaining."

His brow furrowed. "You don't have to entertain me. We don't have to go to bed every time we get together, either." He looked slightly abashed. "We can talk."

Sara pushed her hair back from her face, wishing she weren't having this conversation. "Due to natural technical difficulties, I won't be going to bed with you for the next few days."

He was silent for a while. She saw exactly when the light dawned.

A look of discomfort flitted across his face. Then he shrugged. "Carly used to get cramps and yell or cry a lot."

"So what did you do?"

"I gave her a hot-water bottle and a hug."

Warmth flooded her at the thought. "That was nice."

He shrugged again. "You've got cramps?"

Sara shook her head. "Backache and tears. Not a stellar night, so I'm sure you'll understand if I don't—"

"How about a back rub and a hug?"

She blinked. He'd disarmed her. "I, uh . . ." She was at a loss. "This isn't going to be all that enjoyable."

"It's okay, Sara. I just want to be with you."

His simple declaration touched her deeply. She felt her throat tighten and her eyes brim with tears. "Oh, damn you," she wailed. "Who needs *Dr. Zhivago* with you around?"

"Come here."

"I don't think so." She crossed her arms over her chest.

He came toward her and drew her stiff body into his arms. He felt so good, his clean, musky scent conjuring up memories of the nights they'd shared. She was overwhelmed and overcome, so it shouldn't have been any big surprise when she burst out crying.

He carried her to the sofa and handed her a tissue.

Sara collected herself and blew her nose. "This is so humiliating."

Calmly ignoring her embarrassment, Daniel took off his jacket. "If you lie on your stomach, I can start that back rub."

Sara acquiesced, burying her head in a pillow.

"Upper or lower?" She felt the sofa dip as he sat on it.

"Lower," she murmured.

At the first, firm touch of his hands, she moaned.

"Good?"

"Yessss."

For several minutes he continued to knead the small of her back. Although the massage felt wonderful, Sara felt compelled to protest. "You don't have to do this."

"I know."

"Daniel—"

"Sara, relax. That's all I'm asking from you tonight. You don't have to be sexy, cute, or even too polite. Just relax."

And in spite of herself she did.

After Daniel finished the back rub, he pulled her beside him and wrapped his arm around her. "Do you remember the first time you heard about the birds and the bees?"

Sara nodded. "One of my foster parents gave me a short, vague explanation, but I didn't get all the details until health class in seventh grade. What about you?"

Daniel rubbed his chin against her hair and smiled. "My mother always wanted to be a country-music star."

"Really? My mother wanted to be a Rockette."

They looked at each other and laughed.

"My mother was always making up these crazy songs that didn't rhyme. When it came time to have 'the talk,' she made up a song that described the reproductive process from beginning to end." Daniel chuckled again. "To the tune of 'Amazing Grace.'"

Sara stared at him. "I don't believe you."

Daniel raised his hand as if he were on the witness stand. "I kid you not. I'd swear on a Baptist hymnal."

"What did your father do?"

"My father adored my mother. He would have done just about anything for her, but this was one time when he drew the line. After she sang it to me, he told her that he would take care of 'the talk' from then on. And he told me just to forget I'd ever heard Mama's little song."

"Bet you remember it."

"Word for word. It was . . . unforgettable."

"She must have been wonderful."

Daniel nodded, absently stroking Sara's hair. "She was very passionate about everything she did. She wasn't one for half measures. It was tough for all of us when she died. I used to think it was worst for Carly. She was so little, and she stuttered for a long time after Mama died." He paused, deep in thought.

"But it was worst for my father. It was like someone turned out the light and nothing could turn it on again. I felt sorry for the woman he remarried, even though she could be mean as hell."

Daniel made a face. "Eunice was always on Garth about something."

His family was more important to him than he probably realized, Sara thought, hearing the intensity in Daniel's voice. "What about you?"

"Eunice didn't mess with me. I was old enough, and after Dad died, the farm passed on to me." There was strength and confidence in his voice. Sara imagined a younger Daniel with all that confidence and understood why Eunice had never attempted to usurp his position. "She moved out when Carly was sixteen. I sent her money every month until she died."

"At one time or another I imagine all of your brothers and Carly have looked to you when they needed something. It's amazing that you kept everything together."

Daniel shook his head. "I haven't always come up with what they needed. Like with Garth—" He broke off, remembering a particularly tough period several years ago.

Sara hated seeing the pained expression on his face. "Who did Garth call when he and Erin had problems with the mare?"

"Me," he admitted, and tugged her hair. "And you've heard enough about my family history tonight."

Sara wasn't sure she would ever hear enough.

Daniel fascinated her. Everything she learned about him made her want to know more.

"Did your mother ever go to New York to audition for the Rockettes?" he asked.

"Not that I know of. She stayed in that same little town in Minnesota most of her life. If she hadn't had me, maybe . . ."

"Did she ever say that?" he asked in a low voice.

Sara hesitated. "Daniel, I don't have any cute little stories about songs my mother made up. She was young, alone, and confused. I think she wanted to put me up for adoption, but something inside her wouldn't let her. And after all these years I'm not sure if that would have been better or not. I was jerked from one foster home to hers for a little while and back to a different foster home. I would have loved to have had one home, one person I could have been sure of, but there wasn't anyone. Stability will always be important to me. I think that's why I got . . ." She winced, unsure if she wanted to reveal anymore.

"Married?"

Sara nodded. "I found out there's a difference between physical stability and emotional stability. Big difference," she murmured.

Daniel paused for a moment, watching different emotions flow across her face. He wished he knew what stirred those emotions. He wished he knew so much more about Sara. "What was he like?"

"He was older, a lawyer with grown children from his first marriage. He seemed lonely." She gave a faint smile in remembrance, and Daniel felt a pinch in his gut. "I wouldn't go out with him at first, but he was so nice about it that I felt guilty. In the beginning he was easy to be with. I felt comfortable with him, and he didn't place any demands on me. When he asked me to marry him, I thought I'd feel secure. And I did, in a way, that first year."

"But something changed after the first year," he concluded, because she didn't look happy.

Sara pressed her lips together. "Yes. He found out about some of my background and—"

Within his arms Sara tensed, and Daniel could feel her distress. He frowned in confusion. "About your mother?"

"Yes." She hesitated and continued. "He also found out from a colleague about another relationship I'd been involved in several years ago before I even met him. He was terribly embarrassed and felt betrayed. Before he was killed in a car accident, I think he was considering a divorce." She cleared her throat, and Daniel could hear the defeat in her voice. "That last year wasn't much fun. He didn't want to be around me." She bit her lip and looked away. "He wouldn't touch me."

Sara must have been devastated. She was someone who craved physical closeness, and Daniel was more than happy to accommodate her need. He tightened his arms around her. "I don't think I would have liked your husband."

"He was a good man, Daniel, well respected by everyone both professionally and personally. He just couldn't handle that I was—"

"Warm, beautiful, and *human*. He wanted a woman with a pedigree and a perfect past. In my opinion he got something better and didn't know what to do with it."

"Don't." Sara shook her head. Tears welled in her eyes. "Don't make me into something I'm not. Don't make *us* into something we're not. I'm the wild woman, and this is your crazy, passionate affair. Don't ever forget that." She drew in a deep breath. "Ever."

NINE

"I'm telling you, Carly, Daniel's acting strange."

Sara heard Troy's voice which carried through the open door of Carly's office, and stopped mid-stride.

"He got in late one night, and when I ribbed him a little bit, he nearly smashed my vocal cords. I don't know what's going on, but it must be some pretty heavy-duty stuff for Daniel to lose it. Has Sara said anything to you?"

"It's not really our business," Carly admonished Troy.

"Guess that means she hasn't."

Sara's breath froze in her throat. Troy's words replayed through her mind—*Daniel's acting strange . . . he nearly smashed my vocal cords . . . heavy-duty stuff.* She felt a rush of panic. Ever since that night when Daniel had come over and they hadn't made love, a new intimacy had bloomed between them.

Amazing what exchanging a few little secrets could do. It had left her feeling naked, raw, and completely open to Daniel. She'd wondered if he'd been similarly affected. Now she *knew* that Daniel was getting in deep enough that it affected his relationship with Troy. She felt a painful twist at the thought of causing a rift between him and any of his brothers. Sara was particularly sensitive to family strife, since she had no family.

Swallowing hard, she struggled with an overwhelming wave of confusion. Should she break off with Daniel? Her heart sank. Could she?

Troy started to say something, but Sara had heard enough. "Carly," she called. "I've got a selection of menus from the new catering service."

She walked through the doorway and immediately saw the guilt in their eyes.

"Hi, Troy. How are you?"

He shifted his glance from Carly to Sara. "Fine. And you?"

How polite, she thought, staring at him in surprise. How unlike Troy. "Fine," she managed, handing the menus to Carly. Lord help her, she needed a clear head. She needed some perspective, and there was no way she was going to get it with Daniel coming over nearly every night. A glimmer of an idea came to mind. "I've been thinking about that extra week of vacation you offered me at Christmas. Would next week be okay?"

"Next week would be fine," Carly said. "I was wondering if you'd actually take me up on it. It's hard enough getting you to take a day off, let alone an entire week."

"Well, it might just be a long weekend," Sara said, considering her options.

Carly's eyebrows rose. "Oh. Any ideas about where you'll go?"

"Nothing firm." That was putting it mildly.

Troy jingled the change in his pocket and looked as if he were getting ready to say something.

Sara looked at him expectantly. Troy had one of those transparent faces that hid neither his thoughts nor his feelings. Right now he reeked with curiosity. "Yes?" she prompted.

He shrugged, jingled some more, and put a forced-looking smile on his face. "Hope you have a good time."

Unprepared for the bland remark, Sara took a moment before saying, "Thank you." If there was one thing the Pendleton brothers knew how to do, she thought, it was to take her by surprise.

She decided against a warm-weather trip to the islands and selected a skiing resort in West Virginia. The exterior of the main building reminded her of a castle. The carpet was red, the service impeccable, and thank goodness there wasn't a snow bunny or ski stud in sight.

The bellman escorted her to her room, and after she sank down on the big bed with a white chenille bedspread, Sara breathed a deep sigh of relief. She appreciated the elegant but comfortable decor of the room with its reproduction furniture, tasteful pastel wallpaper, and floor-to-ceiling windows that offered a snowy, mountainous view that would put any picture to shame.

The ambience totally relaxed her until she caught sight of the violets. Immediately rising from the bed, she crossed the room to the small desk and stared at the lovely arrangement. Tentatively she removed the card and read it. *Thinking of you, Daniel.*

A rush of emotion shook her. She put the card to her lips. "Oh, Daniel," she whispered, "what am I going to do with you?"

Sara remembered when he'd learned she was going away. He'd found the reservation confirmation on her kitchen counter one evening and asked how long she'd be gone. Fighting her awkwardness, she'd told him and he hadn't mentioned it again. He didn't ask if she was going alone. He didn't ask if she wanted him to come along. He didn't ask anything.

He was respecting her privacy, and she should

feel pleased. But for some contrary reason that eluded her, she didn't. Suddenly the room felt too big. The bed was designed for two. The closet would easily hold both Daniel's clothes and hers. Even the bathtub would have accommodated his big body and her smaller one.

Swearing, she put down the card and decided to soak in that bathtub until she could model for a prune commercial. And she would enjoy every damn minute of it.

The following day she spent the morning on the slopes, indulged in an afternoon nap, and took the late seating for dinner. She thanked the maître'd when he placed her near the crackling fireplace in the large dining room. After making her dinner selection, she kept the menu, which not only listed the food but also described the history of the resort. She was reading when the waiter brought a bottle of champagne to her table.

"I didn't order—"

The waiter smiled. "A gentleman sent it as a gift. He would like to join you for dinner."

Feeling awkward, Sara lifted her shoulders. "I really hadn't planned . . ."

The waiter tilted his head in the direction of a small bar. "He's the tall one at the end."

Sara looked up and met the violet-eyed gaze of the man she'd been trying to put into proper perspective. Her pulse kicked into overdrive.

Daniel's mouth slid into a cocky grin. There he sat emanating a confidence that bordered on arrogance, and Sara knew every other woman in the room was probably staring at him in fascination.

She pulled her gaze from Daniel's. "Please tell the . . ."—she hesitated briefly, then continued— "gentleman that I don't dine with impudent men when I'm on vacation."

The waiter nodded, then, looking warily at Daniel, headed toward the bar, the bottle of champagne in his hand.

Sara sipped her water and watched out of the corner of her eye as the waiter gave Daniel her message. Daniel didn't bat an eye. He just laughed out loud, walked straight to the other chair at her table, and sat down.

"I could have you thrown out," she told him. Her physical and emotional reactions to him were immediate. Her blood pumped through her veins, she felt a flush of heat burning her skin, an indescribable joy tighten within her, and she didn't like any of it one bit.

He motioned the waiter toward them. "Honey, if I get thrown out, you're coming with me." Daniel instructed the waiter to open the champagne. He tasted it and nodded. "Good."

Still looking uncertain, the waiter retreated.

"Didn't you say you had several things you needed to take care of this weekend?" Sara ventured. He wore a corduroy jacket over a sport shirt and casual slacks. His eyes glinted with cocky humor, and his hair was attractively mussed. Damn, he looked good.

"There's always something to do on a farm, Sara." He snagged her hand and wrapped his around it. "Ever since I got involved with this wild woman, though, I've finally been doing some things I always wanted to do."

He gave her a look that said he liked doing all those things with her. Sara's stomach danced at the sexual intent in his gaze. "Is that so?"

Daniel nodded. "It is. Do you know how long it's been since I took a real vacation?"

She shook her head. "How long?"

"Seven years. I've got three days and three nights to make up for all that time."

"What possessed you to take one now?"

He leaned forward and lowered his voice. "You didn't really think I'd be able to stand the idea of staying in Beulah when the woman I want is all alone at a ski resort, did you?"

"It was only for four nights, and"—Sara glanced down at the table, then back at him—"I'm not the only woman in Beulah."

"As far as I'm concerned, you are," he said. Then he lifted her hand and pressed it to his mouth.

At that moment Sara lost any perspective she'd gained.

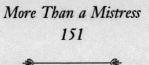

After finishing their meal they walked to the elevators. "My room's on the second floor," Sara informed Daniel.

He pushed the up button. "Mine's on the third."

Surprised, Sara swung her head around to look at him. "I thought you—"

"You thought I'd assume that I would stay in your room?" The doors opened, and he guided her into the elevator. He pushed the button for the third floor. "I may be pushy, but I don't make a lot of assumptions. It's your choice whether you sleep alone or not."

Sara pondered that all the way to Daniel's room. Watching him curiously, she sensed his tension and wondered what had put him on edge. Overbearing yet caring, he was so complex that she hadn't quite figured him out yet. Whatever she did or didn't understand about him, Sara was certain of one thing: She would do whatever she could not to hurt him.

Seven years since he'd taken a vacation, she thought, shaking her head. He'd been too busy being what everyone else needed him to be, too busy taking care of everyone else's needs to take a well-earned break. Determination swelled inside her. If Daniel Pendleton wanted a vacation with her, then she'd damn well give him one he wouldn't forget.

She squeezed his arm as he unlocked the door to his room.

"It's a suite," she said upon entering, impressed with the size. "And I thought my room was huge." She skimmed her hand over the back of the sofa, then peeked into the bedroom. A wall of windows offered a breathtaking view of the mountain, and a gas fireplace was ready to be lit. "I've always had a weakness for fireplaces." She stepped into the bathroom and made an "Oooh" sound of pleasure. "A Jacuzzi."

Leaning against the doorway, Daniel relaxed slightly. He knew he'd taken a risk by showing up unannounced. His brothers had thought he'd gone completely nuts when he'd told them his plans yesterday. Halfway to West Virginia he'd started to agree. What if she'd already met somebody?

Pushing back his uncertainty, he strolled toward her and put his hands on her slim shoulders. "That tub's big enough for two."

"Two? It's big enough for ten."

He laughed. "I wasn't interested in having that big of a party."

Sara became very still. "Were you planning a party?"

"If two people can have a party, yeah." He squeezed her shoulders, then hooked his arms around her. When she rubbed her cheek against his arm, he felt some more of his tension ease. "I'm sending only one invitation. If I can't have a party with this person, then I won't have one at all."

"Sounds like a very private party," she murmured, turning in his arms to face him.

Daniel swallowed. "It will be. The invitation's very specific. I'll do my best to keep my guest happy, but I want her to stay all night."

Sara's eyes grew dark. "All night?"

Holding his breath, he nodded. "I want to do something I've never done before." He leaned forward and matched his forehead to hers. "I want to wake up in the morning with Sara Kingston in my arms."

Sara closed her eyes. "Oh, Daniel."

He swallowed a curse. "Oh, Daniel what?" he asked in a tight voice.

Sara bit her lip and shook her head.

Daniel's heart fell to his knees. He couldn't read her. Her face was saying yes, but she was shaking her head no.

"Yes," she finally said, putting him out of his misery.

He blinked. "Yes?"

"Yes," she repeated, and wrapped her arms around his neck. "But do I get the chocolate the maid left on your pillow?"

She could have asked for a lot more and Daniel would have given it to her.

He lit the fire and ordered another bottle of

champagne from room service while Sara popped microwave popcorn. It was a crazy combination, but the night seemed to call for craziness. Twenty minutes of easy conversation, two glasses of bubbly, and Daniel watched Sara turn delightfully, deliciously tipsy.

Her fingers fumbled with the buttons of his shirt. "Do we dance or go swimming?"

"Swimming?" he asked, letting her fumble all she wanted. It was sheer pleasure to be the single object of Sara's attention.

"In the Jacuzzi." She frowned in concentration and pushed his shirt from his shoulders. "I think dancing first, don't you?"

Actually the bed appealed to him. "How about—" he began, but she'd whirled away from him to fiddle with the radio. She found an easy-listening station and was humming along with a popular tune.

Her gaze fixed on his, she unbuttoned her silky blouse and let it slide from her shoulders to the floor. Her skin shimmered like satin in the firelight, and Daniel's attention was caught by the way her nipples nearly spilled from her sheer, low-cut, bra.

When Sara opened her arms, he went to her and brought her close to him. "I thought you wanted to dance," he murmured, running his lips along her neck.

Sara shivered. "I do."

He unfastened the clasp of her bra. "It's gonna be tough to concentrate on dancing when you don't have any clothes on the top half of your body. I'll be the first to admit I'm very"—he cupped her breasts and groaned—"distracted."

Closing her eyes, Sara pushed herself into his hand, and he felt her nipples peak stiffly against his palms. "You think it's tough to concentrate now. Just wait until the rest of me is bare."

"Ahh, Sara, I'm not sure this is gonna work." He rubbed his aching masculinity against her belly.

"Sure it will," she said breathlessly. "You said you wanted a private party with a wild woman, and that's what I'm going to give you."

"Not—" He wanted to say, "*Not just any wild woman,*" but she chose that moment to kiss him. In the back of his mind he wished he'd never made that comment about wanting a wild woman, because his desire was directed toward a particular woman. And that woman was Sara, wild or not. He needed to make sure she understood that.

But her scent was wrapping around him, her tongue was teasing his lips, and her breasts were rubbing tantalizingly against his chest. She made him feel giddy with desire.

Her hands fluttered down to the front of his slacks.

"Ah, Sara, Sara . . ."

"Keep dancing, Daniel," she whispered, working his belt loose and his zipper open.

He gave a frustrated groan. "Dance?"

As she pushed his slacks and underwear down, she brought his manhood into contact with her stomach, and then, to his utter delight, her breasts. The sight of him hugged tightly within her cleavage was so erotic, his whole body throbbed with arousal.

She pulled away to tug off his boots, and Daniel muffled a shout of despair. Impatiently kicking his clothes off, he twined his fingers through her hair and urged her to her feet. He took time for a kiss that rocked him and made her tremble. With little finesse he pushed her slim skirt and panties past her hips and down her thighs.

Moving in a little wiggle that electrified his body, she stepped out of the clothes. Daniel tried to nudge her toward the bedroom, but Sara shook her head. "We're gonna dance." She interlaced her fingers with his and held their hands out to either side.

Her body swayed back and forth, brushing, teasing his. He was starting to sweat. "This is torture."

Sara rubbed her open mouth over his chest. "Concentrate on the music."

Daniel freed one of his hands and drew her hips closer to his. "Honey, there's only one thing

I'm concentrating on." He bent his knees and slid his hard arousal between her thighs, instinctively searching for her heat and moistness. A half beat later he found the slick, silky notch and swallowed her gasp.

He rocked and thrust against her while she moved in exquisite counter motion. Exquisitely stimulating, exquisitely breathtaking, exquisitely heart-robbing.

"Daniel," she murmured in a trembling voice. Her breath came in little pants against his chest. Daniel felt the warm moistness between her thighs bathing him. He nudged against her opening, wanting nothing more than to slip inside her. His mouth was dry with excitement. "It's time," he said. "Let me—"

She shook her head again and slid down his body, her breasts painting a path of fire down his abdomen, over his jutting flesh, to his straining thighs. "Christ! What—"

He felt her breath on him. She touched him delicately with her lips, caressed him with her tongue, then took him into her mouth. A red mist of excitement fell over his eyes. Cradling him in her palms, she loved him with uninhibited delight, driving him to the brink. He was about to lose himself to her sweetly milking caress when she pulled back and looked at him.

She wanted all of him.

He could tell by the dazed expression in her smoky eyes, and the realization of her intent scorched his soul. It was thrilling to have Sara utterly consumed with his satisfaction. Slowly she glided her tongue up the length of his shaft.

Daniel was caught between feeling helpless and feeling powerful.

She moved her mouth to him yet again, ready to take him over the edge. But in a moment of shattering clarity Daniel realized he craved the ultimate connection with this woman. He turned, and her moist kiss glanced his hip.

Before he could speak, he had to swallow twice over the lump in his throat. "Inside you, Sara. I have to be inside you, baby."

Nodding, she got to her feet and let him lead her to the bedroom. He kissed her thoroughly, his tongue dueling with hers in a prelude to the movements their bodies would make. The fact that she tasted like him made him all the more determined to possess her. He would have traded the farm to be able to slide inside her with nothing separating them, to feel her moist, feminine walls cling to him, and then to experience the vibration of her every tiny inner shudder.

He almost did it. He pushed inside her just a bit to torture himself, but a thin thread of common sense made him pull out. His groans of frustration mingled with hers.

Sara clutched at him. "You're not leaving," she said desperately. "Tell me you're not stopping."

His hands trembled as he removed hers. "One second. Hold on for me. One second."

Daniel nearly ran to the bathroom, where he'd left his shaving kit with the condoms inside. He grabbed a handful and returned to Sara, careful not to look at her. His restraint was so tenuous, he'd never felt so out of control before. He threw the plastic packets on the bedside table, except for one, which he tore open. Only after smoothing on the sheath did he allow himself to gaze at her.

Her hair was a mussed cloud of brown silk, her eyes were dark with need, her lips were swollen from his kisses. Her arms lay at her sides, ready to enfold him in a tender embrace. Her knees were bent, her thighs open so that he could see the very heart of her femininity, the glistening essence of her arousal. Daniel was transfixed by the sight of her, and for several moments stood gazing at her in silence.

"Daniel?" Sara said, a husky catch in her voice that grabbed his heart.

He slowly lowered his body to hers, pressing his hard chest to her soft breasts. "Do you know how beautiful you are?" he asked, entering her in one fluid stroke.

Sara gasped and wrapped her arms around him.

"I know you make me feel beautiful," she whispered.

"I want to be as close as I can get." He pulled back and thrust deeply into her.

There was something humming in the air between them. Something that neither had planned. Something that indicated this went way past sex to something she'd never before experienced. Sara was frightened, but what she felt for Daniel wouldn't let her draw back even to protect herself emotionally.

"More," she pleaded. "More."

Gritting his teeth, he thrust as far as he could. Shudders racked her, but she held on tight to Daniel, his violet eyes her only anchor to this world.

Daniel savored the miracle of Sara coming apart in his arms. They were skin to skin, closer than close, with nothing separating them. He was filled with triumph and awe. He wanted to pause to memorize the expression on her face, but she moved, and her inner muscles clenched around him. The pleasure was so intense, it was nearly unbearable, and his strangled cry mingled with hers as they exploded into another realm.

TEN

The next morning Sara woke slowly. She squinted her eyes at the sliver of light coming through a gap in the curtains. Her cheek rested on Daniel's shoulder with her hair splayed across his arm. Her breasts pressed against his ribs, while her legs twined with his long muscular, hairy ones.

Her palm lay on his chest, and she could feel the pounding of his heart. It seemed to permeate her skin, and she had the sensation of having Daniel in her blood, her brain, her heart, even her soul.

It was such a disquieting notion that she gingerly pulled her hand away. She pushed her hair out of her face and was struck again by how close they were. She could see each individual whisker on his jaw. His kiss-swollen lips were gently parted, and his lashes were a black veil over his eyes.

His hair tumbled over his forehead in appealing disarray.

Entirely too appealing, she decided.

She carefully untangled her legs from Daniel's and, holding her breath, shifted her body. Just when she was sure she would escape without waking Daniel, his hand snaked out and clasped her wrist.

"Mornin', darlin'," he murmured in a sleepy, sexy voice. "Where are we goin'?"

Sara smiled at his use of *we*. "*I* was going to take a bath."

"And now?"

She wondered when he was going to open his eyes. "I guess I'm not going anywhere unless I plan on leaving my left hand with you."

His lips lifted in a grin. "Guess not." With a seemingly effortless flick of his wrist, he eliminated all her hard-won inches away from him and hauled her across his torso.

Then he opened his eyes.

His bright violet gaze knocked the breath out of her.

"Hi, beautiful," he said.

"Hi, beautiful," she echoed.

The memory of the night before connected them like a strand of silk. Its impact showed on his face as it probably did on hers. Silence stretched between them, and she could think of absolutely nothing to say to fill it. Feeling both warm and raw, Sara broke eye contact and looked away. Her gaze caught on the bedside table, where several plastic packets lay cluttered. Humor replaced self-consciousness.

Looking back at Daniel, she smiled. "Were you a Boy Scout?"

He quirked a dark eyebrow. "Yeah. Why?"

She rubbed his rough chin with her index finger. "Don't they have some sort of motto about being prepared? It's a good thing you remembered to bring protection, because I wasn't prepared."

He looked pleased. "You didn't bring anything?"

"No. Why should I?"

He dragged her down for a kiss instead of answering the question. When he released her, he licked his lips. "You don't ever have to worry about protection, Sara. I wouldn't want any surprises." He laughed. "Unlike my brother-in-law Russ."

Sara nodded, recalling a conversation she'd had with Carly just a few days ago. "Carly said he's been dropping hints, but she'd like to put off the experience of having children a little longer."

Grimacing, Daniel nodded. "I think I'd like to put it off forever."

"That makes sense," Sara said thoughtfully. "You've been looking after your brothers and sister for so long, you probably feel you've already had the headaches and responsibilities of families."

"Yeah, and not enough of the pleasures associated with making them." His gaze meandered down to her breasts. "My hand has decided it wants to join yours in the bathtub."

"Oh, really?" Sara laughed. "Just your hand?"

"Well, if you're gonna be greedy," he said in a put-upon voice, "I guess I could let the other hand join you too."

"Such generosity," she said in mock praise. She walked her fingers up his arm and saw goose bumps rise on his flesh. Something else was rising too. She bit her lip to keep from smiling. "Both hands and nothing else? We'll see."

They made it out to the slopes after brunch. Daniel had skied only one time before, so, despite his natural athletic ability, it took him a while to get used to it. After he'd crashed a couple of times in the fresh powder, Sara came to his side and tried to help him back on his feet. He swore under his breath. "This is nuts."

"You could take a refresher lesson," Sara suggested.

He shook his head and brushed snow off his sleeve. "I don't want to waste the time."

Sara didn't think it would be a waste of time, but she kept her opinion to herself.

He looked at her. "Go ahead. What am I doing wrong?"

"You're sure you want to know?"

"I asked, didn't I?"

Sara pointed to his long legs. "You're locking your knees. If you bend them, you'll have enough flexibility to keep your balance. Right now you're too stiff."

"Okay. Bend my knees." He tugged on his ski cap with an expression of renewed determination. "And I always thought women liked their men stiff."

Sara stared at him as he scooted back on track. It took her a minute before she understood his double entendre. She laughed and called after him, "I said your *knees* were too stiff, Daniel. Your *knees*."

The weekend passed in a series of golden moments that Sara knew she would remember for a long time. He coaxed her into staying in his suite, so she moved her clothes from her room to his. Because of their constant proximity, she learned little things about Daniel that she hadn't known before. Such as the fact that Daniel woke up in a wonderful mood. He displayed not a bit of crabbiness; instead he liked to talk and cuddle. She wondered if he'd always been that way. If so, then she understood why his mother had adored him.

If the conversation lapsed more than three seconds past one A.M., he was out like a light. He liked to be touched by her and not just sexually. He would sprawl his big body across the bed and hint that he needed a back rub. When she instinctively took his hand, he never failed to close his around hers. He liked privacy, but he included her in that privacy. When they were in the restaurant or lobby, Sara noticed he tended to gravitate to a quiet cubby or corner.

Their last night at the resort he led her to a little place away from the crowds, where they drank Irish coffee and admired the lighted view from the window.

From the booth next to them came a woman's raised voice. "That's all? It's been a lot of fun, and you'll always remember this weekend? I thought this was more than just a fun weekend, Tom."

Sara heard the woman's distress and looked around for an unobtrusive way out of the nook she and Daniel shared. There was none, she realized, cringing. She hated to eavesdrop, and this kind of conversation would have been conducted best in private. Carefully avoiding Daniel's gaze, Sara studied her mug of coffee.

"Carrie, I told you from the beginning that I'm not interested in getting tied down." The man's voice was unemotional. "I had a good time and made sure you had one too. Don't make it into something it's not."

"I guess I'm just not as good at meaningless involvements as you are, but I can take a hint. It's over. Excuse me while I pack."

Sara's heart twisted at the woman's pain. Then she gave a sigh of relief at the sound of retreating footsteps.

Daniel gave a low whistle. "That was sticky."

Sara nodded. "I guess good-byes often are."

Daniel shrugged.

Silence descended between them, and Sara couldn't help but see a parallel between that couple's relationship and her relationship with Daniel. The only difference was that Sara completely understood that Daniel was not interested in commitment. She wondered what would happen when Daniel's interest in her waned. Her heart sank at the thought.

"You're awfully quiet," he said, wrapping his hand around her shoulders. "What are you thinking about?"

"That couple."

"Yeah. It left a bad taste in my mouth."

"Their ideas about their relationship were obviously worlds apart. He didn't seem to have any problem saying good-bye. I guess it made me wonder . . ." Sara hesitated, thinking this was an uncomfortable discussion.

"Wonder what?" he prodded.

She swallowed past the hard knot in her throat. "Well, I guess I wonder how *you* say good-bye."

Daniel looked at her as if he'd swallowed a lemon. "Why the hell would you wonder that?"

Feeling defensive, Sara moved away from him. "Just curious, I guess. I mean, I'm sure you've ended relationships before, and I was curious about how you handled it."

Daniel looked distinctly ill at ease. "It usually isn't a big deal because I make sure from the very beginning that the woman understands that I don't want marriage. The difference between me and that guy is that I make sure that's what the woman wants too."

"And it's never gotten sticky?"

"Maybe once or twice," he admitted.

"What do you do then?"

He gave a long-suffering sigh. "I explain that the woman needs a man who wants the same things she does. A man who is ready to make a commitment deserves her love more than I ever could. I tell her she has my respect and that the man who gets her will be one lucky son of a bitch." He swore in frustration. "This has got to be the most awkward, unromantic discussion I've ever had with a woman. Why are we talking about this on our last night here?"

"I guess because overhearing that couple made me wonder how you said good-bye. And then I thought it might be a good idea to prepare myself for that eventuality, since we have a similar no-strings arrangement."

Daniel stared at her in disbelief. "You mean you've been talking about us?"

Sara was confused. Her feelings were a jumble of hope and fear. "I don't know who I was talking about."

He stepped closer and put his hands on her shoulders. "Sara, the only thing I'm interested in ending between you and me is this crazy discussion. As far as I'm concerned, we just got started."

"It's been a month," she pointed out with a sad smile. "And crazy, passionate affairs with wild women don't last forever."

Daniel heard the ominous message in her words. It hit him square in the gut. Somewhere along the way his intentions toward Sara had begun to change. It may have happened after that first night they'd spent together. It may have happened during any number of other special moments they'd shared. He wasn't sure when it had happened. He only knew it had, and now he was stuck with the rules he'd originally set up between them.

He'd gone along content in his ignorant assumption that he had control of their relationship. He pulled the strings. He set the limits. Now he realized she could sever the tie between them and leave him flat. The notion caught him off guard. He sifted his fingers through her hair. "Works both ways," he admitted, though it cost him. "You could say good-bye too."

Sara's eyes widened as if the thought hadn't occurred to her. Daniel cursed himself. "Now I've given you an idea I don't want you thinking about. What do I do now?"

For several moments she looked at him, then she gave a slow smile. "I once heard that if you're thinking about something you don't want to think about, then you need to replace that thought with a different one."

"So?"

Her hands skimmed up to his shoulders. She gave a little shrug that had his heart jumping. "So I guess you need to give me something else to think about."

Hope soared in his chest as he lowered his head. "I'll do my best."

And heaven help her, he did.

The next morning they loaded up her car and his truck. Sara lamented the fact that they had to drive separately, but it was amazing the way a few little things could make such a big difference. She felt protected when Daniel warned her to drive slowly on the snow-packed roads out of the resort complex. They made several pit stops. Every time they stopped, he kissed her, leaving her with a warmth that lasted until the next break.

It was late when they reached her house. After a lingering kiss at her door Daniel left for the farm. Sara might have felt lonely, but Pavi was beside himself with delight when she walked in. He alternately howled and licked her for fifteen minutes straight.

Over the next week and a half Daniel visited her every other day and called her on the days he didn't see her. The pattern afforded them stability, and Sara began to feel the seductive pull of security and something deeper.

The fact that Daniel was so dependable only made him more appealing to her. It was obvious that his desire for her hadn't dimmed in the slightest. It was also obvious that part of the reason he came to her with such regularity was because he simply enjoyed her presence. He seemed to like following her around her kitchen and talking with her about her day or the farm. Their quiet conversations seemed as important to him as his "passionate affair with the wild woman."

With each passing day she felt the boundaries she'd set blur a little more, and the depth of her feelings for him went way past anything she'd ever experienced. It alarmed her, but Daniel's mere presence robbed her of the ability to distance herself from him. Her only discomfort was his continued effort to draw her into his family.

"It'll be fun," he promised as he teased her mercilessly late one night. He gently blew on her puckering bare nipples. They were on her couch, and she wasn't quite sure when their clothes had been discarded. At the moment she didn't really care. Sara was having difficulty following the change in conversation. Just a moment ago Daniel had been making a few more graphic promises. She arched, but he backed away. "What will be fun?" she asked.

He bent closer and darted his tongue across the beaded tip.

"Ohhh." She bit her lip when he drew away again.

"The potluck dinner after church on Sunday."

Before she could automatically say no, he lowered his mouth to hers. His tongue slipped smoothly past her lips to tease and taunt her while his chest pressed against her exquisitely sensitive nipples. A moan escaped her throat.

"I'll take you to church, then we can meet the rest of the family at my Aunt Bitsy's house."

No, no, no, her mind warned, but his mouth was moving from one breast to the other. Sara sucked in a deep breath and shook her head.

Daniel stopped, put his hands on either side of her head, and gently moved it in an affirmative, nodding motion. He looked at her with the confidence of a man who had grown accustomed to getting what he wanted, and what he wanted was Sara.

She tried to steel herself against his effect on her, but it was tough with him nudging her thighs apart and her body turning soft and moist. She closed her eyes and licked her lips. "I don't think—"

"Please," he muttered against her mouth.

No, no, no. Absolutely not, her conscience desperately called. Feeling tugged in two different directions, Sara shut her eyes.

"Please, Sara."

Hearing him say "please" had her resistance crumbling. She took a deep breath, opened her eyes, and looked into his deep violet gaze. She had the sensation of sinking and losing her will. Wanting more than anything to please him, she felt her objections slip through her fingers like sand. "Okay."

Daniel's gaze lit with pleasure, and Sara was torn between joy and fear.

ELEVEN

"So, you're Daniel's girl."

Daniel watched Sara blink at Aunt Bitsy's blunt statement. Feeling her stiffen beside him, he wished he had an inkling of what was going on in her head and why she was so uptight about his family. He reached over and gave Aunt Bitsy a kiss on the cheek. "Give her a break," he whispered, then raised his voice to a conversational tone. "Sara is Carly's assistant. She's been living in Beulah for about a year."

Aunt Bitsy sniffed. "Don't try to change the subject with me, Daniel Pendleton. You've never brought a girl to my house before. That must mean something."

Certain Sara was about to bolt, Daniel tightened his hand around hers and shook his head in frustration. He should have expected this from his crotchety aunt. "Sara, this lovely woman who bakes the best pies in Tennessee is my Aunt Bitsy."

Removing her hand from his, Sara gave him a sideways glance, then turned to the older woman. "My pleasure to meet you, and it's so kind of you to include me in your family get-together."

Aunt Bitsy took Sara's hand. "There's always room for one more at my house. You remember that, you hear."

At that moment Luke rescued them by running to Sara and tugging on her skirt. "I'm gonna be a Pendleton." His face shone with excitement. "And my mommy's gonna have a baby, so I get to be a big brother."

"Erin's pregnant?" Daniel asked in surprise.

"Yes, sir!" Luke was nearly dancing with joy.

Dropping to her knees, Sara gave Luke a hug. For some strange reason she felt a special connection with this little boy. Perhaps it was because, like her, he'd never met his biological father, and up to this point he hadn't been quite a Pendleton either. "Luke Pendleton?" she said with a smile.

Luke's chest puffed out with pride. "Garth asked if he could 'dopt me and if I'd like to call him Dad." He grinned widely, revealing a missing front tooth. "I do."

Her heart squeezed. "How wonderful. Garth is so lucky to have you for his little boy," Sara said.

"Yeah, and I get to be a Pendleton. Maybe you could be a Pendleton, too, if you married Daniel."

Blood roared in Sara's ears. Luke's face blurred before her eyes. *Marry Daniel.* Her breath froze in her lungs. Suddenly it was as if Luke's words were an arrow and her heart the bull's-eye. He'd given voice to a wish so secret, Sara had never even admitted it to herself. It was impossible. It was something Daniel would never want. He valued the limited amount of freedom he had. It couldn't happen, but God help her, she had fallen in love with Daniel and wished she could have with him everything she'd never had.

The realization hit her hard. She thought she'd been so careful. She knew she'd been riding the edge of a very thin line, but she thought she'd held just enough distance to prevent this. The excited chattering of those around her became deafening, making her dizzy. Then she heard Daniel say her name twice. Shaking her head to clear it, she noticed Luke was long gone.

"Sara." Concern colored Daniel's voice.

Careful to hide her deep distress, Sara slowly stood and mustered a smile.

"You okay?" he murmured, putting his hand around her waist.

"Fine," she managed, avoiding his gaze. "Shouldn't we find Garth and Erin so we can congratulate them?"

Carly and Russ came up behind them. "Not one word," Carly said firmly to Russ. "I'm going to kill Garth for this. Now I'll have to put up with hints from you for the next nine months."

Daniel gave a covert laugh next to Sara's ear. "Carly's going to have her hands full now. And look at Garth's face. He looks like a stunned bull."

While the Pendletons celebrated the good news, Sara struggled with the knowledge that she'd made the stupid mistake of falling in love with a man who wanted her in his bed but not in his heart. With a new awareness she watched him as he interacted with his family. This was the man she loved, she thought, this man who slapped Garth on the back and gave Erin a gentle hug. This was the man she could want forever. However, this was also the man she could have for only a while. Perhaps this was why she'd been resistant to joining Daniel in family activities. Perhaps, underneath it all, some part of her had been trying to protect herself from the knowledge that she had grown to love him more than she'd ever dreamed she could.

A shiver of fear passed through her. Acutely sensitive to the turmoil inside her, Sara worked hard to conceal it. By the time she and Daniel left, she felt emotionally exhausted.

On the drive home Daniel reached over and tugged a lock of her hair. "You're quiet. Did we overwhelm you again?"

Sara smiled. "Not too much. It's a nice kind of noisy."

"I can tell you've got something on your mind. Did Troy bug you about something?"

"No. He barely said more than a few sentences to me."

Daniel nodded, feeling relieved. "Am I gonna have to prod this out of you?"

Sara hesitated. "I hope you won't," she said quietly.

Daniel felt the back of his neck tense. "I hate it when you get that polite tone in your voice."

"Would you like it better if I were rude?"

Daniel answered without hesitation. "Yeah, I would. I want the real Sara, good and bad. Kiss me or curse me, but give me the real thing."

Sara crossed her arms over her chest. "I believe I've already given you the real thing."

Daniel heard the slightest edge in her voice and grinned. "So you have. But the strangest thing happens every time you give yourself to me. It just makes me want more. I want to get into every crack and crevice of Sara Kingston. I want to know what scares you, what makes you cry, what you want to hide." He shifted his truck into third gear. "And why."

"That wasn't part of the bargain."

"Then let's renegotiate."

"No," she said flatly.

Instant frustration stung like salt water on an open wound. He wanted her open to him, completely open. He wanted to read her like a book, every word, every sentence, every chapter that was Sara. It wasn't enough to have her in bed. He'd become addicted to her quiet charm and secretly tender heart. He felt the need to protect at the same time that he wanted the right to all of her. Not just body but mind, heart, and soul. The need was powerful and overwhelming in its intensity. And he realized, it couldn't be denied.

It changed the color of things. This wasn't just his crazy, passionate affair anymore. It had become much more.

But at times Sara was like a tightly shut clam. Now was one of those times. Taking a deep breath, Daniel wondered where his usual supply of patience was. "Okay," he muttered, looking at her as he braked at the stoplight. "For now." Because he hated the thought of any distance between them, he pulled her closer and kissed her possessively. Her mouth was soft and sensuous and willing, and he tasted her until he felt her body start to respond to him. Lifting his head, he stared into her dazed eyes. "Your eyes change colors when I kiss you," he said roughly.

Sara took a deep breath. "My whole body changes colors when you kiss me."

He chuckled, rubbing her soft chin with his

thumb. "Guess I'll have to check that out when we get back to your house."

"I guess you will."

A car horn beeped behind them, reminding Daniel that the light had changed. He accelerated, opened the window to let in some cool air, and decided to change the subject. "What'd you think of Garth and Erin's news?"

"They seemed surprised, but happy."

Daniel shook his head. "It's hard for me to imagine Garth settling down and having kids. But I guess I shouldn't look a gift horse in the mouth. Now that Russ and Carly and Garth and Erin have made sure the Pendleton line continues, I can forget about that duty with no sweat."

Ten days later Sara learned she was pregnant. "We always used protection," she heard herself say to the doctor in a thin voice. "Always," she whispered.

He slipped his glasses on his nose. "Your chart indicates that you are single."

Sara nodded. God help her, was her heart still beating?

"Are you frightened about being a single parent?"

Sara nodded again. "How did this happen?" she

burst out. "We used condoms every single time. *Every* time."

The doctor sighed. "Only abstinence is one-hundred-percent effective. While condoms are currently popular since they offer additional protection against sexually transmitted disease, the figures pertaining to contraception indicate that they have a ten-to-eighteen-percent failure rate." He lifted his hand. "If condoms are used improperly, the failure rate increases. Not to be droll, but all it takes is a pin-sized hole and . . ."

"And I'm pregnant," she concluded hoarsely. A pinhole in a rubber and she was pregnant. Sara wondered if that was how it had happened, because as wild as their lovemaking got, she and Daniel were meticulous about protection. She remembered one time they'd abstained because there'd been no contraceptive available.

Her blood ran through her veins like ice water. She lifted a trembling hand to her mouth. "I'm pregnant."

"It's very early. You have plenty of time to come to grips with this." Wearing a serious but thoughtful expression, he continued. "You have options. There are adoption agencies." He hesitated. "And if you decide that you don't want to continue the pregnancy, I can refer you to a clinic. You do have options," he repeated.

His words swirled in her brain. *Options.* God

help her, what was she going to do? Sara swallowed and tried to compose herself. She laced her fingers around the straps of her purse. "I'm going to have to—" She cleared her throat and blinked hard. "I'm going to have to think about all this." She shrugged. "Is there anything I'm supposed to do? Or not do?" Sara bit her lip. She knew nothing about being pregnant.

After the doctor gave her a few instructions about taking vitamins, eating correctly, and avoiding alcohol and caffeine, Sara murmured a vague acknowledgment and walked out of the office.

That evening Sara fed Pavi and nibbled on a sandwich. Recalling a suggestion her counselor had given her some years back, she pulled out a piece of paper and sketched out her situation. She was so confused, she couldn't write fast enough to get all her feelings down.

She wasn't even certain she should tell Daniel. He would take responsibility, insist on marrying her, help raise the child—and probably regret it every day of his life.

Bowing her head into her hands, she felt her numbness wane and her eyes burn. A lump formed in her throat. *Options.* She was filled with doubt and uncertainty. Should she tell Daniel? Should she marry him if he asked her?

Not if he asked out of his deep sense of responsibility and obligation. Not if he didn't love her. And how could she know for certain now?

Could she go through nine months of pregnancy and give up a baby?

Did she possess the fortitude to go to that clinic and end her pregnancy? Sara swallowed. She'd always thought of abortion as a political issue or some other woman's choice. She'd never thought she'd be in a position where she would have to consider it herself.

Her head began to pound. Choices she didn't want to make. None of them seemed right.

The question that taunted her more than anything, though, was could she be a mother? Could she be a good mother, or was it a situation of like-mother, like-daughter? Her heart squeezed at the thought. Sara wasn't sure she had the right stuff to raise a child by herself. She certainly hadn't been given an adequate example to follow.

Tears welled in her eyes. Sara crumpled up the piece of paper and threw it across the room. She'd settled nothing and she'd never felt so alone in her life. Alone. And scared.

By the following evening she'd reached two major conclusions. She wasn't telling Daniel right away, and she wasn't going to see him until she'd settled something in her mind. She had her excuses all lined up, and because Daniel was distracted by some problems at the farm, Sara got away with it for five days.

Five days, five pieces of paper, and she still had no answers. She was beginning to run out of excuses.

"I haven't seen you in five nights, Sara," Daniel said.

"I know. We've both been busy."

"I can bring over some dinner and wine, rent a movie if you want."

Sara's chest tightened. "I don't think so. I'm a little tired tonight." That was the truth. She now had three symptoms of pregnancy. She was tired, her bladder seemed to have shrunk, and her breasts were tender.

Daniel sighed. "Then I'll watch you sleep. I just need to see you."

Sara closed her eyes. At the very heart of her being she needed to see Daniel, too, to have him take her in his arms and reassure her that she didn't need to worry, that everything would be okay. She also knew, however, that for her own peace of mind she needed to reach a decision and make some plans. "I'm sorry," she finally said, "but I think I need a little space."

Dead silence settled on the line. Sara heard Daniel take a breath.

"Space," he repeated in a deep, lethally calm voice.

Sara's panic rose to the surface. "I've got a lot on my mind. I can't really explain it, but—" Her voice cracked, and she swallowed hard. "There are some things I need to think about."

"I don't like the sound of this."

"I'm sorry." She patted Pavi. His silky hair offered a little comfort in this comfortless situation. "I don't like it either. It's—"

Daniel's voice sliced across hers. "When can I see you?"

Sara bit her lip against the loss of his gentleness. Even before she opened her mouth, her words tasted bitter on her tongue. "I don't know."

Sara waited, dreading his response.

"Good-bye, Sara," he said quietly, then hung up.

A cold, hard knot formed in her chest, making it hard to breathe. His words had sounded so final. God help her, she didn't want to lose him. The knot clenched painfully. Her whole body seemed to rebel at the thought. Pavi even sensed her distress, whining and rubbing against her hand.

Though she hovered near tears, Sara tried not to overreact. She took deep breaths and attempted to reason with herself. It took thirty minutes, but she finally managed to calm herself. She was sipping herbal tea when the doorbell rang.

Her hands immediately began to shake. She knew who it was. Setting down the tea, Sara made her way across the room and opened the door. He wore jeans and a denim jacket, and he looked tired and unhappy. She wanted to put her arms around him and soothe away the tiredness. She wanted to make him smile. Instead she made herself stand by the door.

Daniel didn't wait for an invitation, since he suspected he might not get one. He walked through the doorway into Sara's den and turned to face her. "Are you gonna tell me what's going on?"

She crossed her arms over her chest, and Daniel noticed she had faint circles under her eyes. She looked vulnerable, beautiful, and miserable.

"I can't," she confessed. "I just can't."

His gut tightened at the desperate sound in her voice. "This sounds serious."

She looked down and bit her lip. "It is. But it's something I've got to figure out for myself. I don't know how my future will be affected and—"

"Future?" Daniel narrowed his eyes. Something was going on here, and he didn't like the direction the conversation was taking. He had the unsettling impression that Sara might be pulling back permanently. The notion was completely unacceptable to him. He walked closer to her and tilted up her chin, urging her to meet his gaze. In her eyes he saw pain and secrets. Both made him restless. "Is this your way of brushing me off?"

"No," she answered immediately. "But I'm not sure what's going to happen with me."

He saw the sheen of tears glistening in her eyes

and swore, then folded her into his arms. "Honey, why can't you tell me?"

"I can't. Please don't ask me to. I just need a little time to figure things out." She snuggled deeper into his embrace.

The only thing that gave him any comfort in this situation was the way she was clinging to him as if she never wanted to let go. Wishing he could do more, he stroked her hair in a soothing gesture. "How long do you need?"

She breathed deeply and pressed her cheek against his chest. "I don't know."

"I don't know" was too vague. He wanted this situation over and done with. He wanted Sara back even if she was hurting. The several days he'd already gone without her felt too long, as if something vital had been missing from his life. The realization of how much she'd come to mean to him shook him. He swallowed hard. "I'll give you a week. Is there anything I can do?'"

"Just hold me for a few minutes," she said, her voice muffled by his shirt. "Please."

Daniel wrestled with the odd feeling that she was asking him to hold her for the last time.

Sara spent the week evaluating her choices. Sometimes the pregnancy seemed surreal, as if it weren't really happening to her. Her body hadn't changed in any measurable way. For the most part she didn't feel any different. But she never forgot it, not during her waking or her sleeping hours when she dreamed about it.

She forced herself to consider all her options. It was incredibly difficult, and the pro-and-con lists didn't work quite so well with her emotions so involved. One by one she eliminated her choices. She didn't think she had the strength to carry a baby for nine months and put it up for adoption, although she admired those women who did.

She wondered if she was a wicked person to consider ending the pregnancy before she got too attached to the idea of having Daniel's baby. But she was already attached. And the idea of having Daniel's baby. But she was already attached. And the idea of losing her baby frightened her.

With each passing day it was becoming clearer that she would have this baby and, God help her, raise it with all the love and care she could muster. It was also becoming clear that Sara might have to move away from Beulah County.

On day seven, D-day, Sara sat at her desk wondering what in the world she could say to Daniel.

Carly put a mug of coffee in front of her. "I'm worried about you."

Sara managed a slight smile. "Thanks. It's nice to know you care enough to worry."

Carly lifted a dark eyebrow. "I'm not the only one. Daniel has called every night this week to ask how you are. Since you haven't confided in me, I haven't been able to tell him much."

Sara looked down at the papers on her desk. "I haven't really confided in anyone yet," she confessed. In a way Sara wished she could talk about her problem with Carly, but since Carly was Daniel's sister, it didn't feel right. "I've gotten myself into a situation that will necessitate some big changes and I needed to make some decisions."

Carly sat on the corner of the desk. "And have you?"

Sara nodded slowly. "Some."

"Do you mind telling me how this could affect me or Daniel?"

"I might not be staying in Beulah County."

Carly's eyes widened. "Why not?"

"It might be best."

"Not for me it wouldn't. And I'm sure Daniel wouldn't want you to leave."

Sara sighed and looked directly at Carly. "You've been a great boss and an even better friend, but there are some things about my past that I never told you. Things that might change your opinion of me. I can't begin to tell you how much I care about Daniel, but I'm trying to do what's best for everyone."

"I don't give a rip about your past, and I bet Daniel doesn't either." Carly frowned. "There's obviously something else going on here. Something you're not ready to talk about. I wish you felt you could, but I can respect your privacy if you promise not to do anything rash without telling me first."

Sara knew she wouldn't leave without first telling Carly, so the request was no problem. "I promise."

Carly nodded. "Okay. And one more thing."

"What?"

"I'm taking you out for an early dinner after work tonight. You look too pale."

Sara thought about her seesaw appetite. "I don't know—"

Carly pressed her hand over Sara's. "You're making me feel helpless. If you won't talk to me, at least let me feed you."

Appreciating the comfort of Carly's friendship, Sara relented. "Okay, but I've got to get home early." She wondered if she'd be able to eat a thing. Dread wove through her stomach. After dinner Daniel would be waiting for an explanation.

TWELVE

Responsible, mature, even-tempered Daniel Pendleton was ready to throw a fit. He slammed the receiver down and swore. This was the fourth time he'd called Sara and gotten her answering machine. He prowled from one side of the den to the other, muttering under his breath.

Troy made a noise and slunk farther into the sofa cushions.

"Did you say something?" Daniel asked sharply.

Shooting Daniel a wary glance, Troy shook his head. "Not a word. I was clearing my throat."

Daniel jammed his hands into his pockets and brooded.

"I take it Sara's not home," Troy said cautiously.

"You take it right."

"Have you tried Carly or Russ?"

"No." He'd been too intent on Sara to call his sister tonight as he had every other night this week. "Good idea, Troy," he said, heading for the phone.

From Russ, Daniel learned that Carly had taken Sara out for dinner at a local restaurant. He waited fifteen more minutes and grew tired of cooling his heels, so he headed for the restaurant. Under normal circumstances he'd feel foolish, but he'd spent the entire last week racking his brain about what could be upsetting Sara so much and he'd come up empty.

Empty was how he'd felt when he realized he couldn't hold her or make love to her or talk with her. A few nights ago he'd nearly gone nuts just wanting to hear her voice or smell her skin.

Drumming his fingers on the steering wheel, he sat in his truck for a few minutes and watched the front door. He chewed his way through a whole pack of mints, all the while wondering if he should have worn more aftershave. Leaning his head back, he closed his eyes. He hadn't ever been this nervous about a woman. Never. Not with his first date nor with his first lover. Funny thing, though, he felt as if he'd learned the true meaning of the word *lover* only with Sara.

His edginess grew too big for the cab. He stepped out into the brisk winter night, and after pacing off his restlessness next to the brick restaurant, he leaned against the wall outside the door.

She walked out, and his heart stopped. She was talking to Carly and she didn't see him at first, so he said her name. "Sara."

She stopped mid-stride, her expression a mixture of surprise and apprehension. "Daniel."

He cleared his throat. "It's been a week."

Sara nodded. "So it has." She turned to Carly and murmured, "Thank you."

Carly squeezed her shoulder and shot Daniel a warning look. She walked away and elbowed him in the ribs to get his attention. "Watch your step, big brother."

After that confidence-building remark, Daniel considered throwing Sara over his shoulder and hauling her back to his house with no discussion. He exhaled in frustration. "You want to go for a ride?"

"Okay."

He helped her into the truck and headed for the lake. They made the entire trip in silence. He caught sight of her hands clenched together in a white-knuckle grip and felt his uneasiness mount. After he pulled to a stop and cut the engine, he covered one of those small, tense hands with his and intertwined their fingers together. He felt the connection. It was more than sizzle and fire. It was warmth and affection, and everything that Sara had become to him.

"Have you got something to tell me?"

She looked out the window. "I've tried to find a good way to tell you this."

Despite his hurt, he was growing tired of her reticence. Suddenly all the strain he'd felt from the week overwhelmed him. His patience snapped, and he released her hand. "How about 'It's been fun, but it's over'?"

Sara jerked her head around. "I wasn't going to say that."

He arched an eyebrow. "No? The words might be different, but the message is the same. Did you finally get bored with the farmer?"

Sara felt as if she'd been slapped. "No! I haven't been bored with you since the first minute we met. This is about something else."

"Sara, I've been in bed with you every night I could manage for the last six weeks. We got closer than close. I can read your face, baby." His gaze slid down to her chest. "I can read your body. Can you tell me that you're not trying to tell me good-bye?"

Unable to deny it, she fell silent. She saw a flash of aching vulnerability in his eyes and felt a stabbing sensation cut through her.

"Well, I guess that says it all." He got out of the truck and slammed the door behind him.

Full of frustration and her own gripping pain, Sara stared after him. She hadn't wanted to hurt him. That was the point of all this, wasn't it? It was why she'd decided to leave Beulah and raise the baby somewhere else. She didn't want to burden him. It had been the hardest decision of her life, and she was scared to death, but she had never wanted to hurt him.

She went after him. His hands were in his pockets, his back to her as he stared into the black night. "I'm sorry," she said softly.

"Why didn't you just tell me instead of jerking my chain all week?"

"This hasn't been easy for me."

He gave a snort of disgust. "You could've fooled me."

Sara felt tears spring to her eyes. "You have no idea how hard this is for me."

He cocked his head to one side, and the light from the moon revealed his clenched jaw. Then he turned around. He hooked his thumbs in his pockets and strutted toward her until he stood an inch away. His face was hard, his eyes unhappy. He was all hurt and anger mixed with the inherent power he wore like a second skin.

The combination seared her heart and soul.

He narrowed his eyes. "Prove it."

Sara's heart raced. "Prove what?"

"If this is *so* hard for you, then prove it."

His gaze was predatory in a way she'd never seen in him before. Her mouth went dry. "What do you mean?"

"I want one last time with you." He rubbed her lower lip with his thumb. "One last wild time when I watch you come apart and feel myself pumping inside you." He lifted her hand and held it against his chest. "You always liked my body, Sara. You always liked the way I kissed you." He shifted his hand to her breast. "You always liked my hands and mouth on you. Do you like the farmer enough to give him one last time?"

Sara sucked in a quick breath of cold winter air. To her dismay her nipple puckered immediately, and she felt a shattering swell of arousal. "This isn't a good idea. It's not what we need."

Daniel slid his hands beneath her coat and circled her waist. "Don't tell me what I need, darlin'. I've gotten used to having you, and it's gonna be hard as hell for me to quit cold turkey."

He lowered his mouth to hers for a kiss that turned her knees to liquid and provoked a visceral tension within her.

"So tell me, babe," he muttered in a rough I-gotta-have-you voice, "do I do anything for you anymore?"

Sara closed her eyes against the need that hummed through her blood. "This is insane, Daniel. We're breaking up."

He covered her mouth with his fingers. "No. No more talk of breaking up tonight. Tomorrow's soon enough. I want to know if I can still make you moan. I want to know if you ever feel like begging as much as I have."

He undid the buttons on her blouse, pushed open the silky material, and slipped his palm over her breast. Sara gasped at his speed and the shot of cold air.

Rubbing her nipple between his thumb and forefinger, he gave a gruff sound of approval. "I always liked your breasts, Sara. They're so sensitive to my hands, just like you are."

Every touch of his fingers against her nipples made her more and more restless. "Daniel," she pleaded, unsure of what she wanted anymore.

"What do you want, honey? Do you want my mouth?" He nuzzled her neck. "You always liked that. Or do you want to say no? It's a little word. Easy to say. You say it a lot. But not to me. If you don't want me, just say no."

She'd never seen him this way, taunting and teasing. Maybe it would have turned her off if she hadn't seen the hurt in his beautiful eyes and heard the hint of desperation in his voice. His pain mirrored her own. Familiar, warm, and strong, his body pressed against hers was the sweetest agony. For all his macho cockiness Daniel was miserable. And she was too. She felt a sudden surge of greed.

What could one more time hurt? It wouldn't change anything in the long run. It wouldn't alter the course she'd chosen. But maybe they could help each other through one last dark night.

Something inside her broke free. She met his gaze straight on. "You know I can't say no to you, Daniel."

She barely blinked before he picked her up and carried her to the truck. After shoving the seat back, he slid in the passenger side, and his mouth fell on hers with primitive hunger. Distantly she was conscious of the door slamming.

Her head swam with the scent of him. Somehow everything felt different, as if their civilized coverings had been stripped off. There wasn't an ounce of hesitation in him. His hands were determined and purposeful. His mouth was an instrument of seduction and possession. This was no gentle, loving good-bye. It was a blatant demonstration of his need for her.

Sara felt a desperation to give and to take. Knowing this was the last time made it worse. She was totally sensitized to everything about him, the friction of his hair between her fingers, the scent of his aftershave, the distinctive minty flavor of his mouth. His warmth wrapped around her more effectively than the coat he'd pushed from her shoulders. When he pulled his mouth from hers, Sara buried her face in his neck, tasting his skin. She felt like a mass of bare nerve endings. Everything was too much, but not enough. And nothing was intimate enough.

He slid his hands under her skirt, and her temperature shot off the thermometer. She rubbed her thighs together to assuage the heavy ache between them.

His tongue scored a trail down her neck to her breast, where he took her nipple between his teeth. Sara jerked. Her breasts were more sensitive than usual.

Daniel paused. "Too rough?"

She shook her head, amazed at the surge of arousal that bucked through her. She was immediately needy. With another flick of his tongue she was near completion.

"You've got great breasts, Sara. Full and tender." Daniel savored the sensation of her nipple in his mouth, sucking deep and long. He felt her body stiffen. "You like that, baby? You like the farmer's mouth on you?"

"Yes. Oh, God!" Her voice was breathless and filled with shock.

Daniel felt her climax. He watched her throw her head back with a deep shudder that tore through her, and he experienced enormous satisfaction knowing he had brought her so far so quickly. It fed more than his ego. It pulled at his heart. His loins throbbed with need, but it was addicting to watch her rapture, to feel her come undone.

She bowed her head to his shoulder, and he slipped his hands past her thigh-high hose and lace panties to her core.

"Daniel," she whispered.

"You're wet. You feel like silk, and I want to taste you."

The mere thought of that intimacy stopped her heart. Sara was still so aroused, she wasn't sure she could bear it.

Daniel swore in frustration. "There's no room. My hands will have to do. Tell me, Sara, do you like the way my hands feel on you?" He eased a finger inside her and pressed his thumb back and forth over her sensitive bead.

Sara cried out. "What are you doing?"

Daniel's voice deepened. "I'm just making sure you don't forget me." Then he leaned forward and kissed her. His tongue plunged in the same mesmerizing rhythm as his finger, and soon Sara was scaling the jagged cliffs again.

He palmed her breast and it was too much. She went over the edge, brokenly calling his name. Tears seeped from her eyes as she struggled to catch her breath and equilibrium. Clinging to him for strength, she felt exquisitely seduced and vulnerable. Something inside her snapped, and suddenly nothing less than him, all of him, would do for her.

Daniel saw the sexual glitter in her eyes as she opened his shirt apart and ran her hands over his chest. Her touch was the match that lit the dynamite. And she had become his ultimate satisfaction.

In the cramped confines of the cab she wove her special version of show-and-tell with her hands and mouth. "You're so strong," she whispered, "so incredibly strong."

She managed to make him feel humbled and ten feet tall at the same time. The knowledge that this was the last time hovered in his mind. Desperation trickled in, but he pushed it away. Sara was here, now. Later he'd find a way to make her stay. Later, God help him, he'd have to.

He sifted his fingers through her hair and watched her slant her eyes seductively at him. She slowly swirled her tongue across his nipple.

Daniel sucked in a quick breath. He didn't know what affected him more, the touch of her tongue or the sensual expression on her face.

He shifted in the seat and undid his belt and the top button of his jeans. "Touch me."

His low-voiced demand was like lightning in the charged atmosphere of the cab. Sara felt as if she had only this moment to bring him all the pleasure she could, this moment to give him everything. She vacillated between the rush of his blatant arousal, her own consuming desire, and the pain that pricked her skin like thorns. She eased down his zipper and slipped her hands inside his jeans to cup his masculinity.

Daniel gave a guttural sound of pleasure. "You've got great hands, Sara."

Sara took those great hands and rubbed and stroked the length of him until the back of his shirt stuck to him with damp perspiration. It was the pleasure of a lifetime to feel her adore him with her fingers. Her hair was disheveled, her eyes dark pools of arousal, and her breasts jiggled and swayed with her slightest move. Daniel was straining toward heaven.

She rubbed her thumb over his honeyed tip and lifted it to her tongue to lick. Daniel groaned. Suddenly his arousal grew more painful. "In my pocket," he muttered.

Sara found the packet and opened it, but instead of putting it on, she lowered her head and took him fully into her mouth.

Daniel swore. "Oh, Sara! God, that feels good." He felt himself swelling so much, he wondered if he would burst out of his skin. He held her head still for a moment, because the pleasure was so intense, he felt the tension in every part of his body.

Sara slowly lifted her head. Her gaze was warm and intimate, but honest. That was one of the things he craved about her, her honest need for him. "I like the way you taste," she whispered.

Daniel closed his eyes and shuddered. It took him a full minute to get a grip on his self-control, but every time he looked at her, he felt himself losing it all over again. "I want to be inside you, Sara," he said in a low, rough voice. "As deep as I can get."

She put the condom on a little too slowly for him, and in his desperate haste Daniel ripped her panties. He positioned her over his swollen masculinity, and inch by excruciating inch Sara took all of him inside her.

He shifted beneath her and watched her mouth form a lovely O of pleasure. Her broken gasp was the only music he'd ever need. Feeling himself stretch and throb, he wrapped his hands around her rear end to adjust her movement. Her undulations provided just enough friction to make his whole body tense for his release.

Daniel licked his dry mouth and stared into Sara's eyes. "You know what makes me weak for you?"

"What?" she asked in a husky voice. She lifted her hips and slid down his shaft again.

Daniel let out a hiss of breath between his teeth. Rocking beneath her, he watched her eyes turn hazy, the way they always did right before she climaxed. "The way you just can't seem—oh, God." She robbed his voice and breath with her tiny internal clenches. He growled, fighting his completion. He was determined to tell her, to make her see that she would have this with no other man and he with no other woman. "The—way"—he swallowed, feeling the first steaming surge—"you can't resist me."

Wild and fierce, he crested and clung to her with all his strength and with his every secret hidden weakness.

Sara cuddled into his chest, a damp, limp puddle of spent femininity still intimately connected to him. Feeling a need to protect her and maintain their closeness, Daniel wrapped his arms around her. She trembled beneath his touch.

"Cold?" he asked, wondering why he always felt he'd been part of a cataclysmic explosion after he'd made love with Sara.

"Not really," she murmured.

He scooped up a handful of hair. "Aftershocks?"

Sara let out a long sigh. "Probably."

They huddled silently amid the scent of their lovemaking and the gradual slowing of their heartbeats. Then Sara tenderly kissed his throat and disentangled herself from him. Daniel was reluctant to release her, but he watched as she slid into the driver's seat and tried to put her clothes in some kind of order.

He did the same with his, and as the silence lengthened between them, he felt the return of his uneasiness.

Covering her hand with his, he tugged her closer. "I lied. I don't want this to be the last time."

Her face clenched in pain, and she dropped her gaze from his. "I thought you didn't want to discuss this tonight."

"It's nuts for us to be apart. You want me and I want you. It's more than sex, but God help me, Sara, I've never felt like I've gotten struck by lightning when making love except with you. And I know you feel the same way about me."

Sara stiffened her resolve. After their incredible lovemaking she felt utterly exposed and defenseless. She felt a connection that ran true and deep. It was made more powerful by the fact that she carried his child. She would give Daniel anything. In her heart that was what she yearned to do, yet she knew she had to stand firm. It would be the most difficult thing she'd ever done. "Feelings aren't everything. There are other considerations." She shook her head in frustration. "Besides, we always knew I wasn't right for you. I told you I didn't want to ruin another good man, and Daniel Pendleton, I damn well will *not* ruin your life."

Daniel stared at her in complete confusion. "What in hell are you talking about?"

Sara expelled a harsh breath, and despite the protest from her heart she forced herself to click into another mode. Bracing herself, she forced herself to begin the good-bye. "Okay. You're always wanting to know my secrets. I told you about my husband, but I never told you what made him turn away from me, did I? I never told you that when I was eighteen, I became the mistress of a married senator in Minnesota." She saw the look of disbelief in his eyes. "Oh, yes, I did. And Daniel, I liked it. I liked the attention. I liked the expensive gifts. He liked teaching me about sex." She paused and swallowed hard over the hard lump of regret in her throat. "And I liked learning."

Daniel closed his eyes and turned his head. Sara could feel the beginning of his rejection of her. It hurt. Lord, it hurt more than anything she'd ever experienced, but she knew it was necessary. He needed to know, and Daniel was too decent not to feel complete repugnance for her when she finished.

"The senator had a very nice family. Two sons and a daughter. His wife was ill, so when he needed a woman, he came to me. The only problem was that the press found out." Sara looked down, remembering the shock and pain again. "Can you guess what he did?"

Daniel said nothing, so she glanced up. "Go ahead, Daniel. Guess what he did."

"I don't know," he muttered quietly. "Did he dump you?"

How she *wished* he'd done that. How she *wished* the man had possessed the sense to dump her.

"He committed suicide, and everyone knew why. Everyone knew he had a mistress, and everyone knew my name. People in Tennessee tend to ignore Minnesota politics, so after a few years I thought I'd shed the bad press. But it always catches up with me. Always. Even if people don't learn by rumors, men seem to sense it. You did."

He jerked his head up to stare at her.

"You knew what you wanted from me from the very beginning. You wanted a passionate affair with a wild woman. You wanted a mistress."

"It's been more than that," he said angrily. "And I never asked you to be my mistress."

"I'm not going to argue semantics with you. You're missing the point. I agreed to see you on your terms. I—wanted you too."

"If you think want is all there is to it, then you're not just wild, you're crazy. I—"

"No!" Sara sliced her hand through the air. She was terrified of hearing him talk about his feelings. There was no way she could finish this if he said the things she'd dreamed of hearing. "Don't you dare say that to me. Do you really think I can believe it now? You've had dozens of opportunities before. Why now?"

Sara turned her head away from him and stared straight out the windshield. She concentrated hard on holding back the dry sob that threatened to break her voice. "I'm getting into the passenger seat and I want you to take me home. You asked me for one last time, and I gave it to you. I gave you everything—" She squinted her eyes at the slight waiver in her own voice and drew in a shallow breath. "Everything I could give. If you won't drive me, I swear I'll walk."

"Sara."

Emotionally wrought, she begged God to make him stop. "Take me home."

THIRTEEN

Around three A.M. Daniel figured out that he never should have taken Sara home. He was still sitting in his truck, remembering her face and smelling her scent. Her eyes had been so empty, it was as if she'd crawled into herself to hide from him; she'd been like brittle spun glass. Her movements had been jerky as she'd left the car. She hadn't looked at him, but she'd managed to whisper, "Good-bye."

And Daniel had felt stunned and lost. His own motions, when he'd started his truck and driven home, had been automatic. His body performed the actions, but his mind was back at the lake with Sara.

He knew he should have told her how he felt about her earlier, but he'd never been good at discussing his feelings. And maybe, just maybe, he hadn't wanted to face how much she'd grown to mean to him. When he thought back over the last several weeks with her, he realized that once she'd let him into her life, she'd never turned him away, not even when he'd shown up uninvited during her vacation. She'd always been there to listen to him and make him feel good. For the most part he'd initiated every time they got together. It underscored her inference that she'd been his mistress.

That stuck in his craw. Had she been right?

"Hell, no," he said out loud. If she'd called, he would have come in a New York minute.

He hit the steering wheel with his fist. A bitter pain throbbed in his chest. He hurt. It wasn't just a tingling little scrape. It was a monstrous, engulfing pain that seemed to take over his whole body. And it went deeper. It was almost as if his very soul were weeping. He didn't want to lose her. Sara had given him something he needed, some elusive, indescribable something that he'd learned to crave once he'd been around her. She was incredibly caring. When she gave herself, she held nothing back. He wondered if she realized how precious that was to him. Just being in her presence gave him a sense of peace he'd never had.

He slumped his head into the cradle of his hands. It would be time to get up and get to work in a couple of hours. Spring was just around the corner, and there was plenty to do. But Daniel just didn't have the stomach for it. Sara Kingston had slipped inside and taken his heart, and he didn't want his heart back. He wanted her.

Lifting his head, he took a deep breath. He'd shouldered many burdens in his life, but nothing had ever felt as heavy nor as cumbersome as the prospect of not having Sara to talk to or touch. There was too much left unsaid between them, too much he hadn't said. It was the challenge of a lifetime to find the right words. It would damn well probably take him the rest of the night. He felt his will harden like steel inside him.

By tomorrow morning, he decided, he was going to pay Sara a visit, and this time she would listen.

Sara turned the washcloth over and slapped it on her forehead again. She was clammy and weak from her first bout of morning sickness. She'd called Carly and told her she hoped to be in by lunchtime.

Lunch. She grimaced. At this point she never wanted to eat again. When Carly had asked about Daniel, Sara had given a vague reply. But he stayed in her mind. He didn't so much whisper through her thoughts as stomp, leaving ripples of vibration and every heart-jerking emotion known to womankind.

Sara ached for him, and for the first time she wondered if she carried his son. Another Pendleton heartbreaker with naughty violet eyes and the will of ten men. Heaven help her. She traded the image of Daniel's face full of disappointment with one of Daniel holding his son in his arms, full of adoration. It was sheer fantasy, but Sara needed anything but the truth this morning. Truth was the fact that she'd permanently severed her relationship with Daniel last night. Truth was that she'd destroyed any chances for a future with him. And the truth was that she felt more lost and more alone than she'd ever felt in her life.

She'd have to face up to the truth soon enough. For now she felt as if she were in mourning, but she needed a way to get through the day, and the fantasy of Daniel's smile provided the way.

Holding him close in her mind, she shut her eyes and drifted asleep until the sound of the doorbell woke her. Turning her head, she glanced at the clock and noticed it was nearly one. It was probably Carly checking on her.

Sara eased out of bed and was pleased to find her equilibrium restored. She didn't bother looking in the mirror. After the physical and emotional turmoil of the last twenty-four hours, she could imagine how she looked.

Pulling open the door, she lost her equilibrium all over again when she saw Daniel standing on her doorstep holding a bunch of violets. The sight of his big strong hand clenched around those fragile little flowers made her throat knot and tears spring to her eyes.

Daniel immediately looked alarmed. "It's not the violets. Tell me it's not the violets."

Forcing her gaze away from the dainty flowers, Sara sniffed and blinked, determined not to cry. Why was he here? "I don't feel very well," she managed, and took a deep breath. "I'm not up to talking."

She started to close the door, but he caught it with his boot. "Tough." Then he shoved it open and walked straight into her living room.

"You have a bad habit of coming into my house when you're not invited," she said to his back.

He turned and met her gaze with frightening resolve. "Better get used to it." He tossed the violets on the end table and unzipped his suede jacket.

Sara's heart took a plunge. Daniel's strength wasn't in his charm. It was in his tenacity. He didn't win by persuasion. He won by wearing the other person down, and right now Sara didn't think she had far to go before she hit rock bottom. "If I'm not in Beulah County, I won't have to get used to it."

He lifted his eyebrows in surprise. Then he narrowed his eyes, and if possible, his look of determination increased. "Thinking of leaving, Sara?" he asked in an ominous voice.

"Yes. I'm thinking about it." Her own voice was far more firm than her convictions were.

"I'll track you down."

"I don't know why."

"Because I love you."

His words hit her with the impact of a steam engine. Sara sucked in a quick breath and shut her eyes. "I told you not to say that last night," she said weakly. She felt his hand on hers.

"You told me lots of things last night. Now it's my turn to tell you."

Panic tumbled through her stomach, making her nauseous. She shook her head and made herself look at him. "I don't want to hear it. Especially now. I really don't feel well."

Daniel saw the desperation in her eyes. It gave him pause. She did look ill, pale, and wan, with shadows beneath her lovely eyes. His mind automatically clicked to the possibility that Sara wasn't just temporarily ill. She could be seriously sick. Daniel's gut tightened in dread. He picked her up, and despite her protest he carried her to the sofa. "How sick are you?"

"Just a little."

His jaw clenched. "Sara, how long have you known that you're sick?"

Sara stared at him. "What do you mean?"

He fought an avalanche of frustration. Getting information from her was harder than trying to till a straight row when he was blindfolded. Right now he felt as if he was wandering around in the dark without a clue, and he was ready to lose every bit of self-control he'd exhibited for the last thirty-five years of his life. "Have you been to a doctor? Are you seriously ill?"

Sara paused, and her gaze flitted away. "I've been to a doctor, and I'm not terminally ill, if that's what you're asking. I don't have a disease or anything like that."

He felt a measure of relief, but was still unsatisfied with her response. She was hiding something, and he was getting close to finding out what it was. "When did you go to the doctor?"

"A couple of weeks ago. This really—"

"Why did you go?"

She glared at him. "To get birth control pills."

His surprise made him hesitate a couple of seconds. "And did you?"

"I don't like being interrogated and I don't want to talk about this." Sara tried to get out of his lap, but Daniel held her firmly.

He smiled grimly. "Tough. You wrapped me around your little finger, then threw me out like yesterday's garbage. Well, honey, let me tell you something. I think you feel a little bit more for me than you've let on, and I sure as hell know I feel more for you than I've ever told you. So until we get this settled to my satisfaction, I'm sticking to you like glue. If that means moving in, I'll do it."

Sara paled. "You're crazy."

"Then you're responsible for me being crazy. Did you get the pills?"

"No." Sara shook her head. "Let me up."

Intent on getting to the bottom of this, Daniel ignored her request. "Why didn't you?"

Sara's face grew tight with anger. "Let me up."

"Answer my question," he said with the persistence of a battering ram.

"No," she repeated.

"You owe me an answer."

Her eyes widened. "I owe you nothing!" she yelled. Struggling with a host of emotions, she pushed hard and stumbled from his lap. "I gave you everything I had."

Daniel was silent less than a moment. "Not enough. Not forever," he said softly. "And I want forever."

Turning away, Sara crossed her arms over her chest. Her heart was pounding, her mind was reeling. This was what she'd wanted. This was what she'd secretly dreamed of. In dark, sleepless hours this was what she'd prayed for.

She almost wanted to tell him, to share the reality of her pregnancy with him. The mere thought of it made her sag with relief. The mere thought of it also made her tremble with terror. Sara opened her mouth, but no sound came out. To her utter shock she couldn't tell him. She'd programmed herself to complete silence about the baby and she couldn't seem to find the words. Desperate, she swept into the kitchen, with Daniel at her heels. She pulled out a stack of papers and thrust them into his hands. "There."

He looked at her, his forehead wrinkled in confusion, then he glanced at the papers. "Adoption. Pros and cons." He flipped to another page, and by the expression on his face, she could guess which one. He looked at her in amazement. "You're pregnant."

Her heart twisted at the flat tone of his voice. Tears filled her eyes. "Yes. Isn't it thrilling?"

His gaze flicked over the papers again. "We always used protection."

"Ever hear the story about the hole in the condom?" Sara's voice was shaky, but she was determined to get this out. "I guess one of yours slipped past quality control."

Stunned, Daniel stared at her in a daze. He was so shocked, he couldn't see straight. "Pregnant?"

Sara swallowed hard. She felt relief and fear at the release of the secret. "Yes. If you look through the papers, you'll find a pro-and-con list for telling Daniel. The con side won. You said you wanted to know my secrets. Well, you can find out just about anything you want to know about the past few weeks if you read them."

She felt worse than if she'd just taken off all her clothes in front of a crowd. Sara wanted to leave.

She didn't care where she went. She'd take her bedroom, the bathroom, a closet, a crack in the floor. All she knew was that she didn't want to stay there. She turned to leave, and Daniel came out of his fog and slipped his hand around her wrist.

"I don't want to read it, Sara. I want to hear it."

She stared at his hand enclosing her narrow wrist. She felt so utterly fragile. Her heart constricted. "Oh, Daniel, please don't make me do this. I feel so weak, I'm afraid I'll cry. And I don't want to watch you be strong when you're really disappointed. I don't want you doing the right thing when you'd rather not. You've been burdened with major responsibilities your whole life. I don't want to add to them."

"The only thing that's been a burden to me is figuring out how to ask you to marry me and get you to say yes."

"See!" she wailed. "There you go, doing the right thing."

Daniel swore. "What can I say to convince you? Give me the right words." He lifted both her hands to his chest and tilted her chin so that she would meet his stormy gaze. "I love you. You've made me feel like life's a treat instead of a drag. You've made me forget every other woman on the planet. I've never been with anyone who made me want to make promises and keep them." Daniel swore again. "You think I'm strong, but I'm not, Sara. Not when it comes to you. When it comes to you, I'm drowning in all these feelings I have for you." He lowered his voice. "And I'm scared you're gonna leave me flat.

"Now, wasn't that romantic?" he said in a self-deprecating tone. He sighed heavily. "I'll protect you till my dying breath. I'll do everything I can to help make you happy. I'm in awe of you. Damn. I wrote all this stuff down last night, and it sounds like crap now. Help me out, Sara. I'm no good at love out loud."

Sara blinked. His pulse pounded against her palms, and her heart squeezed so tight, she could barely breathe. *No good at love out loud?* She felt ready to faint. Sara swallowed. "I think," she said in an unsteady voice, "you lost me after the part about making promises and keeping them."

"Why didn't you tell me you were pregnant?"

Sara looked down. "I was so afraid, Daniel. I'm still afraid. I don't want you to see me as another burden. You have enough as it is. From the very start it was different with you. I tried to keep a distance, and before I realized it, I'd fallen in love with you. And I don't mean a little crush. I mean through-good-and-bad, sickness-and-health kind of love. You'd made it clear that you wanted me for fun. Remember, I was supposed to be your wild, passionate affair?"

Her words were music to his ears. For the first time in thirteen days he felt a ray of hope. "Well, tell me something. If you love me and I love you, then why can't the wild, passionate affair go on forever? Why can't we add a couple of gold rings and promises I feel like I've already made to you and move in together?"

Her expression was so sad, his confidence went straight down the tubes. "Because it won't be just me and you," she explained. "There'll be somebody else. And I'll get big and fat and grouchy. And when the baby cries all day, you'll be grouchy because I'll be too tired to try to be sexy."

"I can't imagine you not sexy. It's not possible."

Sara rolled her eyes. "It's possible. And you haven't said anything about the baby."

"I'm not going to," he said, taking her by surprise. "You dropped a bomb on me last night, then hightailed it out before I could come to grips with it. You've had two weeks and"—he pointed to the papers on the kitchen table—"a tablet of paper to work through the idea that you're pregnant. The least you can give me is a few days. I'll tell you now, though, Sara—nothing you've ever told me could change the way I feel about you. Nothing in your past. Nothing in your present. And nothing in *our* future. It didn't take me long to figure out that you'd put the worst possible slant on your relationship with that senator. You want to deny it?"

Stunned, she could only shake her head. How could she deny the truth? How, she wondered, had he come to know her so well?

"Let's get this settled once and for all. I *hate* the idea of you being with another man. Do you hear me? I *hate* it. And maybe you hate the idea of me being with another woman."

"Yes," she said tensely.

His gaze softened. "As far as I'm concerned, Sara, there's no other woman for me than you. And that means past, present, and future."

Sara took a deep breath, and the words from her heart spilled out. "There's no one else I want to be with, either, Daniel. No one."

Daniel closed his eyes for a long while. Then he opened them and lifted an unsteady hand to her cheek. "It feels so good to hear you say that out loud, but, Sara, you don't have to say a damn thing. It's written on your face. It's in your every touch, every smile."

She felt the sting of tears in her eyes. She was completely overwhelmed. "I thought my little bombshell had done the job," she said in a husky voice.

"You thought wrong."

Sara shook her head at the implacability in his words. His full acceptance of her tarnished past amazed her. "You are an incredibly exceptional man."

"Then I deserve an incredibly exceptional woman." He leaned down and gently kissed her nose. "You."

She wanted to say he deserved better, but something inside her had begun to shift. His belief in her had nudged a hopeful belief in herself. Maybe, just maybe, she was the kind of woman he needed. Sara held her breath and clung to the seed of hope.

"I'm waiting for my answer."

Sara bit her lip. She wasn't ready to say yes. She needed time to absorb all this, time to accept, if she could, that she could have what she'd always dreamed. "This is too fast."

"Not for me. Give me your answer."

Lord, but this man was demanding when he made up his mind. Sara made her own demand. "Give me some time to catch my breath."

"Alone?" Daniel frowned. "You just had a whole week."

Sara smiled, feeling heat rise to her cheeks. "No. I'd rather not be alone."

Daniel's gaze darkened with a suggestion of seduction. He rubbed his thumb over her mouth. "You know, when it's all said and done, I can't resist you. My only saving grace is that you can't seem to resist me either," he murmured in a deep voice that made her think of all the intimacies they'd shared.

Sara nodded.

"And you know I'll wear you down."

Sara felt the beginning of a smile. It started deep inside, where she kept her most secret dreams, and worked its way out.

He gave a heavy sigh. "Okay, Sara, I'm giving you fair warning. I'll do whatever it takes to get a yes from those lips. Do you understand me?"

Sara nodded, and Daniel took that mouth of hers in a mind-melding, heart-binding kiss. And later that afternoon he confessed a few secrets of his own, one of which was his fantasy about Sara in a red silk slip.

Late one night Sara awoke to find Daniel watching her from across the room. Earlier he'd called to tell her that he would be late, and she'd fallen asleep waiting for him. Sara couldn't imagine anyone she'd rather see when she woke up. He was leaning against the doorjamb to her bedroom and he'd stripped off his shirt. Nestled in his hand were a few violets. Sara's heart turned over. He was so beautiful to her that sometimes it hurt to look at him.

In the light from the hall his gaze latched onto hers. "You're pretty when you sleep."

"You're beautiful when you breathe," she returned, and watched him caught between delight and self-consciousness.

He walked to the bed and sat next to her. Then he slowly lifted his hand and placed it on her stomach. "Think it'll be a little girl?"

Her chest tightened at the intimate gesture. It was the first time Daniel had brought up the baby since she'd told him a week ago. "I wondered if it would be a stubborn little boy with violet eyes."

"Stubborn?" he repeated with a quirk of his eyebrow. "Who would he get that from?"

"The same person he'd get the violet eyes from," she replied dryly. "It's a Pendleton trait."

He gave her hair a quick tug and handed her the violets. "I've been thinking about our baby."

Scared, Sara tried to keep her voice calm. "You have?"

He nodded. "You know, I told you how being with you changes the way I look at things. And I gotta tell you, with anyone else, having a baby would be a drag. But with you—"

Sara gave up on calm. "With me what?"

Daniel looked sheepish. "It sounds corny as hell. But with you it feels like an adventure. Do you realize that I like my brothers more now that you're a part of my life? It's like you've come in and changed everything around." His gaze met hers in wonder. "But all you did was love me."

Sara was so moved, her heart felt as if it were flying. "Oh, Daniel." She lifted his hand to her mouth. "I was so worried. Worried that you would

resent me, that you wouldn't want a child, and—"
She bit her lip.

Daniel sensed her deep vulnerability, her battle against fear and anguish. "Tell me," he coaxed. "Tell me."

"I wonder if I'm going to be able to cut it as a mother." Her voice wobbled as she unleashed the hidden fear. "You know what they say about the apple not falling far from the tree."

He leaned closer to her. "Hon, that apple's already fallen far, far from that tree." He looked into her doubt-filled gaze and tried to will his belief into her. "Look at the difference you've made in my life and Carly's. And now we're going to have a baby, and you're gonna love him or her. And I'm gonna love that baby too." He squinted his eyes against a burning sensation. "Don't be scared, Sara. We're going to have an adventure, and I'll be right by your side the whole time."

A change came over her face. Suddenly she radiated hope and love. He thought of how her spirit was a pearl that had formed out of years of resistance and pain. Damn if he wasn't getting poetic about her. But perhaps because he knew that Sara had needed to fight against tremendous odds for that hope and love, it affected him all the more. "There's so much good in you that you don't realize it. I swear, Sara, if it's the last thing I do, I'm gonna make you see it."

"You've already made me see it," she whispered brokenly. She put her hands on either side of his jaw, cradling his face as if it were the most precious thing in the world to her. "Daniel, I think it's time for me to say yes."

Daniel's heart twisted so hard, he said to hell with fighting tears and let them slide down his cheeks.

Sara gently tugged his head down and kissed his tears away.

EPILOGUE

The wedding went off without a hitch. Daniel was grateful for how his brothers had acted toward Sara. He knew she'd been a little nervous, but when each of them had kissed her and welcomed her into the family, it had been one more joy in a day that couldn't seem to hold all the happiness that had passed between them.

His brother Brick had seemed a little preoccupied, but Daniel suspected that Brick was hiding a little romance of his own. Grinning at the thought, Daniel pulled his tuxedo tie loose and undid his shirt buttons. He'd like to see a woman turn Brick on his ear. Yes, that would be an entertaining experience. Though not nearly so entertaining, he thought, as being with Sara tonight.

The champagne was in the ice bucket, the chocolates on the pillows, and his bride was in the bathroom. Despite all they'd shared, he still felt a slice of anticipation. He would hold her soon and make love to her. This time they would share more than a bed, they would seal their vows. His body grew taut as he visualized what she would look like on that big bed.

Restless, he prowled around the suite, unnecessarily adjusting the thermostat and dimming the lights. Impatience made his nerve endings stand on end. He started to call her name, but the bathroom door opened, and his bride's sweet, sexy gaze wrapped around his heart and squeezed as she walked toward him. He didn't even try to fight the grin he felt lifting the corners of his mouth.

In her left hand she held a long, fluffy, soft-looking feather.

Daniel began to sweat. Just imagining what she planned to do with that bit of fluff made him wonder if he would survive the night.

Sara flicked the feather back and forth between her breasts in a taunting motion. "Hope I'm worth the wait." Then she shimmied the wispy tuft down the garment that rendered Daniel speechless. He was sure he'd died and gone to heaven.

She wore a red silk slip.

THE EDITOR'S CORNER

The coming month brings to mind lions and lambs—not only because of the weather but also because of our six wonderful LOVESWEPTs. In these books you'll find fierce and feisty, warm and gentle characters who add up to a rich and exciting array of people whose stories of falling in love are enthralling.

Judy Gill starts things off this month with another terrific story in **KISS AND MAKE UP**, LOVESWEPT #678. He'd never been around when they were married, but now that Kat Waddell has decided to hire a nanny to help with the kids, her ex-husband, Rand, insists he's perfect for the job! Accepting his offer means letting him live in the basement apartment—too dangerously close for a man whose presence arouses potent memories of reckless passion . . . and painful images of love gone wrong. He married Kat hoping for the perfect fantasy family, but the pretty picture he'd imagined didn't include an unhappy wife he never seemed to satisfy . . . except in bed. Now Rand needs to show Kat he's changed. The sensual magic he weaves makes her feel cherished at last, but Kat wonders if it's enough to mend their broken vows. Judy's special touch makes this story of love reborn especially poignant.

It's on to Scotland for **LORD OF THE ISLAND**, LOVESWEPT #679, by the wonderfully talented Kimberli Wagner. Ian MacLeod is annoyed by the American woman who comes to stay on Skye during the difficult winter months, but when Tess Hartley sheds her raingear, the laird is enchanted by the dark-eyed siren whose fiery temper reveals a rebel who won't be ordered around by any man—even him! He expects pity, even revulsion at the evidence of his terrible accident, but Tess's pain runs as deep as his does, and her artist's eye responds to Ian's scarred face with wonder at his courage . . . and a wildfire hunger to lose herself in his arms. As always, Kimberli weaves an intense story of love and triumph you won't soon forget.

Victoria Leigh gives us a hero who is rough, rugged, and capable of **DANGEROUS LOVE**, LOVESWEPT #680. Four years earlier, he'd fallen in love with her picture, but when Luke Sinclair arrives on her secluded island to protect his boss's sister from the man who'd once kidnapped her, he is stunned to find that Elisabeth Connor is more exquisite than he'd dreamed—and not nearly as fragile as he'd feared. Instead, she warms to the fierce heat of his gaze, begging to know the ecstacy of his touch. Even though he's sworn to protect her with his life, Elisabeth must make him see that she wants him to share it with her instead. Only Victoria could deliver a romance that's as sexy and fun as it is touching.

We're delighted to have another fabulous book from Laura Taylor this month, and **WINTER HEART**, LOVESWEPT #681, is Laura at her best. Suspicious that the elegant blonde has a hidden agenda when she hires him to restore a family mansion, Jack McMillan quickly puts Mariah Chandler on the defensive—and is shocked to feel a flash flood of heat and desire rush through him! He believes she is only a spoiled rich girl indulging a whim, but he can't deny the hunger that ignites within him to possess her. Tantalized by sensual longings she's never expected to feel, Mariah surrenders to the dizzying pleasure of Jack's embrace. She's fought her demons by helping other women who have suffered but has never told Jack of the shadows that still haunt her nights. Now Mariah must heal his wounded spirit by finally sharing her pain and daring him to share a future.

Debra Dixon brings together a hot, take-charge Cajun and a sizzling TV seductress in **MIDNIGHT HOUR,** LOVESWEPT #682. Her voice grabs his soul and turns him inside out before he even sees her, but when Dr. Nick Devereaux gazes at Midnight Mercy Malone, the town's TV horror-movie hostess, he aches to muss her gorgeous russet hair . . . and make love to the lady until she moans his name! Still, he likes her even better out of her slinky costumes, an everyday enchantress who tempts him to make regular house calls. His sexy accent gives her goosebumps, but Mercy hopes her lusty alter ego might scare off a man she fears will choose work over her. Yet, his kisses send her up in flames and make her ache for love that never ends. Debra's spectacular romance will leave you breathless.

Olivia Rupprecht invites you to a **SHOTGUN WEDDING,** LOVESWEPT #683. Aaron Breedlove once fled his mountain hamlet to escape his desire for Addy McDonald, but now fate has brought him back— and his father's deathbed plea has given him no choice but to keep the peace between the clans and marry his dangerous obsession! With hair as dark as a moonlit night, Addy smells of wildflowers and rainwater, and Aaron can deny his anguished passion no longer. He is the knight in shining armor she's always dreamed of, but Addy yearns to become his wife in every way—and

Aaron refuses to accept her gift or surrender his soul. **SHOTGUN WEDDING** is a sensual, steamy romance that Olivia does like no one else.

Happy reading,

With warmest wishes,

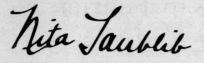

Nita Taublib

Associate Publisher

P.S. Don't miss the spectacular women's novels coming from Bantam in April: **DARK PARADISE** is the dangerously erotic novel of romantic suspense from nationally bestselling author Tami Hoag; **WARRIOR BRIDE** is a sizzling medieval romance in the bestselling tradition of Julie Garwood from Tamara Leigh, a dazzling new author; **REBEL IN SILK** is the fabulous new *Once Upon a Time* romance from bestselling Loveswept author Sandra Chastain. We'll be giving you a sneak peek at these terrific books in next month's LOVESWEPTs. And immediately following this page, look for a preview of the spectacular women's fiction books from Bantam *available now*!

Don't miss these exciting books by your
favorite Bantam authors

On sale in February:
SILK AND STONE
by Deborah Smith

LADY DANGEROUS
by Suzanne Robinson

SINS OF INNOCENCE
by Jean Stone

Deborah Smith

SILK AND STONE

From Miracle *to* Blue Willow, *Deborah Smith's evocative novels have won a special place in readers' hearts. Now comes a spellbinding, unforgettably romantic new work. Vibrant with wit, aching with universal emotion, SILK AND STONE is Deborah Smith at her most triumphant . . .*

She had everything ready for him, everything but herself. What could she say to a husband she hadn't seen or spoken to in ten years: *Hi, honey, how'd your decade go?*

The humor was nervous, and morbid. She knew that. Samantha Raincrow hurt for him, hurt in ways she couldn't put into words. Ten years of waiting, of thinking about what he was going through, of *why* he'd been subjected to it, had worn her down to bare steel.

What he'd endured would always be her fault.

She moved restlessly around the finest hotel suite in the city, obsessed with straightening fresh flowers that were already perfectly arranged in their vases. He wouldn't have seen many flowers. She wanted him to remember the scent of youth and freedom. Of love.

Broad windows looked out over Raleigh. A nice city for a reunion. The North Carolina summer had just begun; the trees still wore the dark shades of new spring leaves.

She wanted everything to be new for him, but knew it could never be, that they were both haunted by the past—betrayals that couldn't be undone. She was Alexandra Lomax's niece; she couldn't scrub that stain out of her blood.

Her gifts were arranged around the suite's sitting room; Sam went to them and ran her hands over each one. A silk tapestry, six-feet-square and woven in geometrics from an old Cherokee design, was draped over a chair. She wanted him to see one of the ways she'd spent all the hours alone. Lined up in a precise row along one wall were five large boxes filled with letters she'd written to him and never sent, because he wouldn't have read them. A journal of every day. On a desk in front of the windows were stacks of bulging photo albums. One was filled with snapshots of her small apartment in California, the car she'd bought second-hand, years ago, and still drove, more of her tapestries, and her loom. And the Cove. Pictures of the wild Cove, and the big log house where he'd been born. She wanted him to see how lovingly she'd cared for it over the years.

The other albums were filled with her modeling portfolio. A strange one, by most standards. Just hands. Her hands, the only beautiful thing about her, holding soaps and perfumes and jewelry, caressing lingerie and detergent and denture cleaner, and a thousand other products. Because she wanted him to understand everything about her work, she'd brought the DeMeda book, too—page after over-sized, sensual page of black-and-white art photos. Photos of her fingertips touching a man's glistening, naked back, or molded to the crest of a muscular, bare thigh.

If he cared, she would explain about the ludicrous amount of money she'd gotten for that work, and that the book had been created by a famous photographer, and was considered an art form. If he cared, she'd assure him that there was nothing provocative about standing under hot studio lights with her hands cramping, while beautiful, half-clothed male models yawned and told her about their latest boyfriends.

If he cared.

Last, she went to a small, rectangular folder on a coffee table near the room's sofa. She sat down and opened it, her hands shaking so badly she could barely grasp the folder. The new deed for the Cove, with both his name and hers on it, was neatly tucked inside. She'd promised to transfer title to him the day he came home. If she hadn't held her ownership of the Cove over him like a threat all these years, he would have divorced her.

She hadn't promised to let him have it without her.

Sam hated that coercion, and knew he hated it, too. It was too much like something her Aunt Alexandra would have done. But Sam would not lose him, not without fighting for a second chance.

The phone rang. She jumped up, scattering the paperwork on the carpet, and ran to answer. "Dreyfus delivery service," said a smooth, elegantly drawling voice. "I have one slightly-used husband for you, ma'am."

Their lawyer's black sense of humor didn't help matters. Her heart pounded, and she felt dizzy. "Ben, you're downstairs?"

"Yes, in the lobby. Actually, I'm in the lobby. He's in the men's room, changing clothes."

"*Changing clothes?*"

"He asked me to stop on the way here. I perform many functions, Sam, but helping my clients pick a new outfit is a first."

"Why in the world—"

"He didn't want you to see him in what they gave him to wear. In a manner of speaking, he wanted to look like a civilian, again."

Sam inhaled raggedly and bowed her head, pressing her fingertips under her eyes, pushing hard. She wouldn't cry, wouldn't let him see her for the first time in ten years with her face swollen and her nose running. Small dignities were all she had left. "Has he said anything?" she asked, when she could trust herself to speak calmly.

"Hmmm, lawyer-client confidentiality, Sam. I represent both of you. What kind of lawyer do you think I am? Never mind, I don't want to hear the brutal truth."

"One who's become a good friend."

Ben hesitated. "Idle flattery." Then, slowly, "He said he would walk away without ever seeing you, again, if he could."

She gripped the phone numbly. *That's no worse than you expected*, she told herself. But she felt dead inside. "Tell him the doors to the suite will be open."

"All right. I'm sure he needs all the open doors he can get."

"I can't leave them all open. If I did, I'd lose him." Ben didn't ask what she meant; he'd helped her engineer some of those closed doors.

"Parole is not freedom," Ben said. "He understands that."

"And I'm sure he's thrilled that he's being forced to live with a wife he doesn't want."

"I suspect he doesn't know what he wants, at the moment."

"He's always known, Ben. That's the problem."

She said good-bye, put the phone down and walked with leaden resolve to the suite's double doors. She opened them and stepped back. For a moment, she considered checking herself in a mirror one last time, turned halfway, then realized she was operating on the assumption that what she looked like mattered to him. So she faced the doors and waited.

Each faint whir and rumble of the elevators down the hall made her nerves dance. She could barely breathe, listening for the sound of those doors opening. She smoothed her upswept hair, then anxiously fingered a blond strand that had escaped. Jerking at each hair, she pulled them out. A dozen or more, each unwilling to go. If it hurt, she didn't notice.

She clasped her hands in front of her pale yellow suitdress, then unclasped them, fiddled with the gold braid along the neck, twisted the plain gold wedding band on her left hand. She never completely removed it from her body, even when she worked. It had either remained on her finger or on a sturdy gold chain around her neck, all these years.

That chain, lying coldly between her breasts, also held his wedding ring.

She heard the hydraulic purr of an elevator settling into place, then the softer rush of metal doors sliding apart. Ten years compressed in the nerve-wracking space of a few seconds. If he weren't the one walking up the long hall right now, if some unsuspecting stranger strolled by instead, she thought her shaking legs would collapse.

Damn the thick carpeting. She couldn't gauge his steps. She wasn't ready. No, she would always be ready. Her life stopped, and she was waiting, waiting . . .

He walked into the doorway and halted. This tall, broad-shouldered stranger was her husband. Every memory she had of his appearance was there, stamped with a brutal decade of maturity, but there. Except for the look in his eyes. Nothing had ever been bleak and hard about him before. He stared at her with an intensity that could have burned her shadow on the floor.

Words were hopeless, but all that they had. "Welcome back," she said. Then, brokenly, *"Jake."*

He took a deep breath, as if a shiver had run through him. He closed the doors without ever taking his eyes off her. Then he was at her in two long steps, grasping her by the shoulders, lifting her to her toes. They were close enough to share a breath, a heartbeat. "I trained myself not to think about you," he said, his voice a raw whisper. "Because if I had, I would have lost my mind."

"I never deserted you. I wanted to be part of your life, but you wouldn't let me. Will you please try now?"

"Do you still have it?" he asked.

Anger. Defeat. The hoarse sound she made contained both. "Yes."

He released her. "Good. That's all that matters."

Sam turned away, tears coming helplessly. After all these years, there was still only one thing he wanted from her, and it was the one thing she hated, a symbol of pride and obsession she would never understand, a blood-red stone that had controlled the lives of too many people already, including theirs.

The Pandora ruby.

LADY DANGEROUS
by
Suzanne Robinson

Liza Elliot had a very good reason for posing as a maid in the house of the notorious Viscount Radcliffe. It was the only way the daring beauty could discover whether this sinister nobleman had been responsible for her brother's murder. But Liza never knew how much she risked until the night she came face-to-face with the dangerously arresting and savagely handsome viscount himself . . .

Iron squealed against iron as the footmen swung the gates back again. Black horses trotted into view, two pairs, drawing a black lacquered carriage. Liza stirred uneasily as she realized that vehicle, tack, and coachman were all in unrelieved black. Polished brass lanterns and fittings provided the only contrast.

The carriage pulled up before the house, the horses stamping and snorting in the cold. The coachman, wrapped in a driving coat and muffled in a black scarf, made no sound as he controlled the ill-tempered menace of his animals. She couldn't help leaning forward a bit, in spite of her growing trepidation. Perhaps it was the eeriness of the fog-drenched night, or the unnerving appearance of the shining black and silent carriage, but no one moved.

Then she saw it. A boot. A black boot unlike any she'd ever seen. High of heel, tapered in the toe, scuffed, and sticking out of the carriage window. Its owner must be reclining inside. As she closed her mouth, which had fallen open, Liza saw a puff of smoke billow out from the interior. So aghast was she at this unorthodox arrival, she didn't hear the duke and his brother come down the steps to stand near her.

Suddenly the boot was withdrawn. The head footman immediately jumped forward and opened the carriage door. The interior lamps hadn't been lit. From the darkness stepped a man so tall, he had to curl almost double to keep his hat from hitting the roof of the vehicle.

The footman retreated as the man straightened. Liza sucked in her breath, and a feeling of unreality swamped her other emotions. The man who stood before her wore clothing so dark, he seemed a part of the night and the gloom of the carriage that had borne him. A low-crowned hat with a wide brim concealed his face, and he wore a long coat that flared away from his body. It was open, and he brushed one edge of it back where it revealed buckskin pants, a vest, a black, low-slung belt and holster bearing a gleaming revolver.

He paused, undisturbed by the shock he'd created. Liza suddenly remembered a pamphlet she'd seen on the American West. That's where she'd seen a man like this. Not anywhere in England, but in illustrations of the American badlands.

At last the man moved. He struck a match on his belt and lit a thin cigar. The tip glowed, and for a moment his face was revealed in the light of the match. She glimpsed black, black hair, so dark it seemed to absorb the flame of the match. Thick lashes lifted to reveal the glitter of cat-green eyes, a straight nose, and a chin that bore a day's stubble. The match died and was tossed aside. The man hooked his thumbs in his belt and sauntered down the line of servants, ignoring them.

He stopped in front of the duke, puffed on the cigar, and stared at the older man. Slowly, a pretense of a smile spread over his face. He removed the cigar from his mouth, shoved his hat back on his head, and spoke for the first time.

"Well, well, well. Evening, Daddy."

That accent, it was so strange—a hot, heavy drawl spiked with cool and nasty amusement. This man took his time with words, caressed them, savored them, and made his enemies wait in apprehension for him to complete them. The duke bristled, and his white hair almost stood out like a lion's mane as he gazed at his son.

"Jocelin, you forget yourself."

The cigar sailed to the ground and hissed as it hit the damp pavement. Liza longed to shrink back from the sudden viciousness that sprang from the viscount's eyes. The viscount smiled again and spoke softly, with relish and an evil amusement. The drawl vanished, to be supplanted by a clipped, aristocratic accent.

"I don't forget. I'll never forget. Forgetting is your vocation, one you've elevated to a sin, or you wouldn't bring my dear uncle where I could get my hands on him."

All gazes fastened on the man standing behind the duke. Though much younger than his brother, Yale Marshall had the same thick hair, black as his brother's had once been, only gray at the temples. Of high stature like his nephew, he reminded Liza of the illustrations of knights in *La Morte d'Arthur*, for he personified doomed beauty and chivalry. He had the same startling green eyes as his nephew, and he gazed at the viscount sadly as the younger man faced him.

Yale murmured to his brother, "I told you I shouldn't have come."

With knightly dignity he stepped aside, and the movement brought him nearer to his nephew. Jocelin's left hand touched the revolver on his hip as his uncle turned. The duke hissed his name, and the hand dropped loosely to his side. He lit another cigar.

At a glance from his face, the butler suddenly sprang into motion. He ran up the steps to open the door. The duke marched after him, leaving his son to follow, slowly, after taking a few leisurely puffs on his cigar.

"Ah, well," he murmured. "I can always kill him later."

SINS OF INNOCENCE
by
JEAN STONE

They were four women with only one thing in common: each gave up her baby to a stranger. They'd met in a home for unwed mothers, where all they had to hold on to was each other. Now, twenty-five years later, it's time to go back and face the past. The date is set for a reunion with the children they have never known. But who will find the courage to attend?

"I've decided to find my baby," Jess said.

Susan picked up a spoon and stirred in a hefty teaspoon of sugar from the bowl. She didn't usually take sugar, but she needed to keep her hands busy. Besides, if she tried to drink from the mug now, she'd probably drop it.

"What's that got to do with me?"

Jess took a sip, then quickly put down the mug. It's probably still too hot, Susan thought. She probably burned the Estée Lauder right off her lips.

"I . . ." The woman stammered, not looking Susan in the eye, "I was wondering if you've ever had the same feelings."

The knot that had found its way into Susan's stomach increased in size.

"I have a son," Susan said.

Jess looked into her mug. "So do I. In fact, I have two sons and a daughter. And"—she picked up the mug to try again—"a husband."

Susan pushed back her hair. *My* baby, she thought. *David's baby.* She closed her eyes, trying to envision what he would look like today. He'd be a man. Older even than David had been when . . .

How could she tell Jess that 1968 had been the biggest regret of her life? How could she tell this woman she no longer knew that she felt the decisions she'd made then had led her in a direction that had no definition, no purpose? But years ago Susan had accepted one important thing: She couldn't go back.

"So why do you want to do this?"

Jess looked across the table at Susan. "Because it's time," she said.

Susan hesitated before asking the next question. "What do you want from me?"

Jess set down her mug and began twisting the ring again. "Haven't you ever wondered? About your baby?"

Only a million times. Only every night when I go to bed. Only every day as I've watched Mark grow and blossom. Only every time I see a boy who is the same age.

"What are you suggesting?"

"I'm planning a reunion. With our children. I've seen Miss Taylor, and she's agreed to help. She knows where they all are."

"*All* of them?"

"Yours. Mine. P.J.'s and Ginny's. I'm going to

contact everyone, even the kids. Whoever shows up, shows up. Whoever doesn't, doesn't. It's a chance we'll all be taking, but we'll be doing it together. *Together*. The way we got through it in the first place."

The words hit Susan like a rapid fire of a BB gun at a carnival. She stood and walked across the room. She straightened the stack of laundry. "I think you're out of your mind," she said.

And don't miss these heart-stopping
romances from Bantam Books,
on sale in March:

DARK PARADISE
by the nationally bestselling author
Tami Hoag
"Tami Hoag belongs at the top of
everyone's favorite author list"
—*Romantic Times*

WARRIOR BRIDE
by **Tamara Leigh**
" . . . a passionate love story that captures all
the splendor of the medieval era."
—nationally bestselling author
Teresa Medeiros

REBEL IN SILK
by **Sandra Chastain**
"Sandra Chastain's characters' steamy
relationships are the stuff dreams are
made of."
—*Romantic Times*

CALL JAN SPILLER'S ASTROLINE

OFFICIAL RULES

To enter the sweepstakes below carefully follow all instructions found elsewhere in this offer.

The **Winners Classic** will award prizes with the following approximate maximum values: 1 Grand Prize: $26,500 (or $25,000 cash alternate); 1 First Prize: $3,000; 5 Second Prizes: $400 each; 35 Third Prizes: $100 each; 1,000 Fourth Prizes: $7.50 each. Total maximum retail value of Winners Classic Sweepstakes is $42,500. Some presentations of this sweepstakes may contain individual entry numbers corresponding to one or more of the aforementioned prize levels. To determine the Winners, individual entry numbers will first be compared with the winning numbers preselected by computer. For winning numbers not returned, prizes will be awarded in random drawings from among all eligible entries received. Prize choices may be offered at various levels. If a winner chooses an automobile prize, all license and registration fees, taxes, destination charges and, other expenses not offered herein are the responsibility of the winner. If a winner chooses a trip, travel must be complete within one year from the time the prize is awarded. Minors must be accompanied by an adult. Travel companion(s) must also sign release of liability. Trips are subject to space and departure availability. Certain black-out dates may apply.

The following applies to the sweepstakes named above:

No purchase necessary. You can also enter the sweepstakes by sending your name and address to: P.O. Box 508, Gibbstown, N.J. 08027. Mail each entry separately. Sweepstakes begins 6/1/93. Entries must be received by 12/30/94. Not responsible for lost, late, damaged, misdirected, illegible or postage due mail. Mechanically reproduced entries are not eligible. All entries become property of the sponsor and will not be returned.

Prize Selection/Validations: Selection of winners will be conducted no later than 5:00 PM on January 28, 1995, by an independent judging organization whose decisions are final. Random drawings will be held at 1211 Avenue of the Americas, New York, N.Y. 10036. Entrants need not be present to win. Odds of winning are determined by total number of entries received. Circulation of this sweepstakes is estimated not to exceed 200 million. All prizes are guaranteed to be awarded and delivered to winners. Winners will be notified by mail and may be required to complete an affidavit of eligibility and release of liability which must be returned within 14 days of date on notification or alternate winners will be selected in a random drawing. Any prize notification letter or any prize returned to a participating sponsor, Bantam Doubleday Dell Publishing Group, Inc., its participating divisions or subsidiaries, or the independent judging organization as undeliverable will be awarded to an alternate winner. Prizes are not transferable. No substitution for prizes except as offered or as may be necessary due to unavailability, in which case a prize of equal or greater value will be awarded. Prizes will be awarded approximately 90 days after the drawing. All taxes are the sole responsibility of the winners. Entry constitutes permission (except where prohibited by law) to use winners' names, hometowns, and likenesses for publicity purposes without further or other compensation. Prizes won by minors will be awarded in the name of parent or legal guardian.

Participation: Sweepstakes open to residents of the United States and Canada, except for the province of Quebec. Sweepstakes sponsored by Bantam Doubleday Dell Publishing Group, Inc., (BDD), 1540 Broadway, New York, NY 10036. Versions of this sweepstakes with different graphics and prize choices will be offered in conjunction with various solicitations or promotions by different subsidiaries and divisions of BDD. Where applicable, winners will have their choice of any prize offered at level won. Employees of BDD, its divisions, subsidiaries, advertising agencies, independent judging organization, and their immediate family members are not eligible.

Canadian residents, in order to win, must first correctly answer a time limited arithmetical skill testing question. Void in Puerto Rico, Quebec and wherever prohibited or restricted by law. Subject to all federal, state, local and provincial laws and regulations. For a list of major prize winners (available after 1/29/95): send a self-addressed, stamped envelope entirely separate from your entry to: Sweepstakes Winners, P.O. Box 517, Gibbstown, NJ 08027. Requests must be received by 12/30/94. DO NOT SEND ANY OTHER CORRESPONDENCE TO THIS P.O. BOX.